Praise for
Walkin' After Midnight

"Joe Ricker is a hard-boiled poet in the tradition of Charles Bukowski. He writes of lonely, scarred men, damaged women, and of haunted places we all know. These shorts are served straight up with no chaser. Like the best of noir, it's about people with few options and often no way out. Highly recommended."
—Ace Atkins, *New York Times* bestselling author

"Tough yet lyrical, bristling with hard-won wisdom, these stories knock you out of any comfort zone you may have found and into the red. Ricker knows people, violence and landscape. He knows truth, too. And these stories beat their fists like drums."
—Tom Franklin, *New York Times* bestselling author

"Joe Ricker's stories are like windows with ragged blinds twisted open to reveal the lives that go on all around us, in spite of us, and sometimes are us. His characters are dark, desperate, and fascinatingly vivid. Read Ricker and have your eyes opened."
—Gerry Boyle, international bestselling author

"This noir collection of short stories announces Joe Ricker as a provocative new talent. His plots swerve and startle as characters emerge from smoky bars, carrying grudges into frozen landscapes. Ricker's style is a turns gritty, raw, and surprisingly tender, while his prose goes down like fine whiskey."
—Carla Norton, *New York Times* bestselling

"Joe Ricker's stories are records of murder and deceit, acts committed by individuals with such considerable damage, and/or in such dire straits, that the actions they commit seem to them logical, and perhaps inevitable. His writing asks us to find empathy where we might otherwise be inclined to turn away."
—Christopher Coake, PEN/Robert W. Bingham Prize

WALKIN' AFTER MIDNIGHT

ALSO BY JOE RICKER

Some Awful Cunning (*)
Porcelain Moths (*)
All the Good in Evil (*)
Still Monsters (*)

(*) – Coming Soon

JOE RICKER

WALKIN' AFTER MIDNIGHT

Down & Out Books
3959 Van Dyke Road, Suite 265
Lutz, FL 33558
DownAndOutBooks.com

The characters and events in this book are fictitious. Any similarity to real persons, living or dead, is coincidental and not intended by the author.

Cover design by JT Lindroos

ISBN: 1-948235-83-8
ISBN-13: 978-1-948235-83-9

*This book is dedicated to my father, Les,
who taught me how to survive
no matter how cold it got or
how little there was to eat.*

CONTENTS

WALKIN' AFTER MIDNIGHT

Before winter sets in, people around here start to get anxious. Crops need to be harvested, and farmers, like the one I work for, push through those bustling days with hopes of turning a profit, which is rare. Most people just break even, like the stones the frost pushes through the earth. Winter comes and freezes the ground, life and the occasional secret. The locals sink into their misery and habits and try not to look at the calendar too often as if they've forgotten that eventually, the ground will thaw, and some secrets will sprout from the darkness.

When I was a kid, right before winter, my dog and I used to bury things together. In the spring, after the first good thaw, we'd head out into the woods and try to find what we'd buried. When the dog died, and it was him I had to bury, I didn't get so eager to push my fingers into the ground after the thaw. I've spent my life burying things, watching them grow and get bigger like a desire that won't stop reaching for light, even in the dark.

It was late fall the first time I saw her. She was in the back of the bar, her ass pushed up against a pool table.

She wore a short green dress the color of moss and lichen, the color blending so efficiently to her as if she were already in the grave. She lifted her leg up on the table and covered the corner pocket with her thigh, leaning the cue in her left hand against the floor to brace herself. The man she was with smashed his mouth against her neck and she tipped the drink in her right hand, spilling it onto the felt. She worked her right foot in a circle and her flat-bottom shoe fell to the marred carpet, which was stained and moist with decades of ignored spillage. The guy next to me muttered about what a whore she was. The people here have a thing for labels, especially concerning other people. In a town like this, people do what they have to, to pass the time, and in the same breath repeat the state mantra, *the way life should be.*

A song came on the jukebox, and she dropped her leg from the table and toed her foot back into her shoe. She pranced around the bar, belting out the lyrics—*I go out walkin' after midnight, out in the starlight, just hopin' you may be, somewhere a-walkin', after midnight, searchin' for me.* She passed a patch of light from the desk lamp the bartender kept by the register. A slightly fat lip made her smile crooked. The edge of her nose beside her eye was bruised, a shade of purple a little darker than her hair. She was good-looking despite that, and she had a better voice, but it was obvious that everyone in there had heard it before. Nothing special, something that wouldn't be missed for a few years until someone heard that song again and asked *Remember that girl who used to sing? Whatever happened to her?* The guy she was necking with smelled the tips of his fingers and smiled. He stuck them in his whiskey and stirred it around.

She squinted her eyes when she sang. For a few moments, I wondered how she got the black eye. She moved closer to me, probably because I was alone, unable to pretend to engage in a conversation topic like the ones around me— the town's deer population problem, high school football, who gave whom herpes. I pulled the brim of my hat lower. I didn't go out to bars much, and I talked to people even less. Something about her kept me posted there against the bar, sipping the lukewarm Labatt that the bartender had on special, two for one.

"Hi," the girl said.

I nodded.

She told me her name, and I'd heard it before in conversations at other bars. She asked for mine.

"Oscar," I told her.

"Like Oscar Wilde?"

"Oscar White."

"What's your middle name?"

"Birmingham."

"Oscar Birmingham White? Sounds like the name of a kindergarten teacher or someone who'll kill the president." The girl repeated my name, and I wasn't fond of the way she did it, snapping her head from side to side and tapping out each syllable on the bar. "You want a shot?"

"No. Thank you."

She ordered two shots of Jameson and pushed one over to me.

"I said I didn't want this."

"I'm a button pusher," she said.

"No kidding."

"Don't be a faggot. Drink it."

I took the shot and let it stick to the back of my throat.

It burned into my lungs and I choked off a gag.

"Have you read any Oscar Wilde?"

I'd read an assortment of his work. I liked him immensely but mostly because he was the only famous person I knew of who shared my name. Another song came on the jukebox as I was about to answer. The girl scrunched her face at me as she started singing and slipped from her bar stool.

The next morning, I woke up earlier than normal. It was still dark when I went out to the fields on Myer's Farm, an organic co-op that milled with vegans and over-zealous, part-time botanists who marveled at the stringy, parched plants they produced. I didn't make much money pulling weeds and pushing seeds, but there's a certain splendor in harvesting something you put in the ground, like a wish that comes true.

I saw the girl a few nights later at a diner where she worked. She didn't recognize me when she slapped a plate of hash and eggs on the table. Her eye was healing, and the swelling in her lip had faded. The eggs were broken, and the hash was cold. In some places, food is a representation of the people who make it.

"You look familiar," she said. "Have I met you before?"

I shook my head.

She bit her lip. "I don't know. There's something about you, but my memory is all fucked up from my car accident." She tapped her pen against her small note pad. "What's your name?"

I took an oversized bite of toast. "Oscar," I answered.

"That's a peculiar name."

"It seems to be. I suppose I'll take that as a compliment."

She shrugged and pulled the check from her apron.

"You're kind of a creeper, aren't you?"

"I prefer 'introvert,'" I told her.

"Puh-tay-toe, puh-tah-toe. You can pay at the register."

I took the check and brought it to the counter when I finished eating. She'd drawn a heart on the back of it and signed her name. The girl went to a different table with a forced smile.

I saw the girl several times over the next week or so. She spent most of her time in a continuous cycle of work, going to the bar and stumbling home or even driving. On some nights I tried to talk to her, but she was always too imbibed or focused on the man who walked her home or tucked her into the front seat of his car.

After a while, it began to present itself to me that I might want to take her home one of those nights, that I wanted to know what sort of pleasure surged through her when a man took her—why she couldn't choose just one. I convinced myself that they couldn't satisfy her, and I began to imagine all the ways that I could, that perhaps I could help her end the turmoil she was obviously suffering.

I managed to be at a lot of the same places she went, and I learned her favorite songs and eavesdropped on her conversations. She'd hopped trains, her greatest passion, and was only a few weeks away before she headed back out on one.

The night we left the bar together I'd been waiting for her to show up. I played an hour and a half of her favorite songs and took the credit for it when she giddily asked who'd played them. She looked happy. I started buying her drinks. She had a shot of whiskey at her fingertips for the rest of the night.

"What are you doing after this?" I asked her just before

the bar closed.

"I don't know. What are you doing, besides being a creeper?"

She had a way of plowing her opinions into the air. I'd seen her get like that toward the end of some of those nights. An anger came from her that was fueled by some dark, hurtful thing in her past that might have allowed her to be a different woman if it hadn't happened. She'd buried things to keep them hidden, secret. I could understand that.

"I was wondering if you'd like to go down to the reservoir. It's a clear night, and there's supposed to be a meteor shower," I told her.

"Yeah? That's cool. I live down by there. You could drop me off at my place."

When we got to the reservoir, I pulled the beer cooler from my trunk. She took one before I had a chance to offer and sat on the hood of my car. Moonlight skipped off the water onto her legs, and I reached out to touch her knee.

"So that's why you brought me out here."

"No. Not really."

"Whatever. Be patient. I want to see a shooting star."

"Are you going to make a wish?"

"Of course."

"What are you going to wish for?"

"For the world to end." She gulped her beer. "What would you wish for?" She looked over at me with a blank expression, her middle finger seductively tracing figure eights on her thigh.

We made love. My pelvis tamped gently against her while she clenched her eyes like it was some sort of punishment. Right before I finished, in the reflection on the windshield, I watched that shooting star she'd been waiting for streak across the sky and I knew that I would never be that guy who asked *Whatever happened to that girl?* I let her slip out from under me and watched her fumble with her pants, pulling them on as if she were dragging some immense weight over her legs. I told her she didn't have to behave the way she did with men anymore, that I could make whatever it was that made her hate herself go away. She got mad at me, yelled and stormed off into the woods. I followed her.

The light of the hunter's moon let through the branches where I knelt over her. She had this cold look about her. Her eyes were cloudy, like a mist had come to settle over the horrible things she'd seen in the world. She looked like she was finally at peace, but there was still a hint of anger in her eyes, betrayal. I didn't speak, just brushed some of the hair from her face and sat there looking at her for a long time. I left before the sun came. I promised myself that in the spring, when the ground thawed, I'd head back out there to see her again.

"Walkin' After Midnight"—Fiddleblack Issue #6 Nov-12

Sarah waited for the slightest fade in the darkness outside, when that first hint of blue pushed up from the horizon, before she crept away from his puttered breathing. All the things she needed were already in place. Her shorts at the hamper, ID and cash in the pockets. Her purse on the chair near the door, and her keys to the Audi parked on the street were exactly where she would leave them—in plain sight of him if he woke up. She made an arc through the house, moving on the balls of her feet, grabbed the shorts and checked the pockets. A yellow shirt and a cap hung on a hook near the door in the kitchen.

She'd come into the world she was leaving with an adoration for the way he'd spoken and touched her, his lips against her ear lobe, his fingers a light, almost secret brush against her face. After time, his distance from her ear grew until there were no words and only the pressure of his knuckles left its echo on her flesh. Outside, she crossed the street to the narrow space between her neighbors' homes. She stopped and pulled a bag of garbage from a trashcan and retrieved her wheeled luggage.

* * *

The sun throws a thin arm of light over the ledge of the horizon, bringing faint color to dim houses. Hours before, when it was still dark, Mr. Wax climbed into the back of the car they would wait in—an Impala with sticky cloth seats that they picked up at the airport when they dropped off the last rental. Mr. Wax didn't fly, and airports were the only place to get one-way rentals. They'd been moving south from Chicago—Indianapolis, St. Louis, Memphis, New Orleans. Four cities in four days, sinking deeper into the rising heat, trading cars in each new city.

Sheldon slides over behind the wheel and watches the sun poke its head into the sky—the radiance of accomplishment. He was half asleep when they got there. He doesn't remember what street they're on, only that they made a turn off Magazine, and then more of them until Mr. Wax parked in front of a pink house with Mardi Gras beads draped over the points of a wrought-iron fence. The street is residential, quiet, much different than the back alleys near the bars they'd lurked before.

This job was special, Mr. Wax told him.

Before the sun peaks over the skyline, a layer of sweat clings to Sheldon's white polo shirt. *Wear simple, plain clothes*, Mr. Wax instructed. *Inconspicuous. Leave your wallet and anything that can identify you*, he said after asking if Sheldon had any tattoos. He didn't. Mr. Wax's faint snoring from the back seat gives him a sense of comfort, like there's a level of respect for his abilities even though Mr. Glenn, Mr. Wax's boss, only ever let him pick up dry-cleaning or run packages to the poker rooms— when they called him *Paperweight* or *Notsobright* or

Special instead of Sheldon.

The heat is heavy and dense around him. Sweat on his body feels like a layer of skin he could peel away. *Heat*, he remembers. Mr. Glenn talked about that with Mr. Wax before they left. He said: *Heat is increasing, and people are getting sloppy. It's time for them to cool off. Head south. Clean up and dump the baggage in New Orleans—as far from us as possible.* They chose Sheldon because no one would see him coming. He could get close.

The only motion on the street is a woman, and Sheldon doesn't see her until long after the wheels of the carry-on she's dragging over brick grabbed his attention. She rounds the corner—a quick, determined pace. Sheldon takes her in, imagines where she's going. He notices her collarbones most, like daggers she could yank away to pierce anything blocking her path.

He thinks about the three men he's killed along the way, the loud gunshot escorting the bullet to whisper through their brain. A final, rapid lullaby. He wonders what their last thoughts were. The first guy's stringent cologne nauseated him before the singe of gunpowder chased it away. He'd never killed anyone, and it didn't seem to affect him. He'd only ever felt present in life, something without purpose, like a stranger at a party people whispered about instead of speaking with. Sheldon tries to remember the interstates they took to get there from Chicago.

A tree-of-life medallion dangles from her neck. She has a narrow waist, short white cut-offs. The taper of her thigh muscles flex in striation close to her hips. *Stems.* That's what they call legs like that. The sleeves of her yellow, collared shirt are rolled up over her elbows. She moves closer, ahead of the plastic rumble. His heart drums movement into the beads of sweat on his chest. A jittery, warm rush crouches inside him. There's a glint of moisture on her temples, a severe gaze in her blue eyes, the *Costa* trucker-hat she's wearing is pulled low.

Sarah makes it to the corner, the rising sun on her back encouraging her movement. Ahead of her, glints of the sun's light ricochet off the shiny particles in the asphalt and the mirrors and thin bands of chrome around windows of the cars she's passing. She wants to check behind her, make sure there's no one following, but that would mean looking back, breaking the first promise to herself. She won't look back, and she'll never fall in love again.

The world has never really made sense to Sheldon, but he wonders in that moment, as he watches the woman pass, about love at first sight—if love can actually happen in milliseconds, less time than it takes for a bullet through the head to kill someone. He's never been in love, never stumbled down that route. He wonders why they chose him. Mr. Wax shifts in the back seat. Sheldon takes in the flex of her calves after she's passed, moving toward the thin canopy of elms. He catches movement in the rearview mirror when he turns back toward the wheel. A sudden electric shudder rolls over him, and Mr. Wax pushes the end of a pistol silencer against his skull.

If you go through the ice, water soaks through the layers of clothes and pulls you down. It forces the air out of your lungs and you drown by the time you hit the bottom and you're gone until they find your body in the spring—if they find your body.

There's no one but us walking on the lake. Falling snow makes it difficult to see the ice shack, four hundred yards out. That's where Louie is waiting for us. That's where the Boss told Louie and me to bring Jimmy because I vouched for Jimmy. And Jimmy owes too much money.

When we were kids, Jimmy fell through the ice in the middle of Square Pond where the water was thirty feet deep. The cold water and the sudden pull downward came, and his face turned the color of the chunks of ice he'd broken through. I lunged and caught his hand. His fingernails dug into my palms. He begged me, and God at the same time, to save him as his head dipped under and he choked on mouthfuls of water. I could feel the toes of my rubber boots sliding over the ice as the weight of him and his drenched layers pulled me toward the hole. My fingers clawed at the ice until Jimmy, somehow, shucked off his boots and bottom layers and kicked and I pulled until we were lying on the ice, panting and scared.

This lake is deeper. Jimmy walks a few feet in front of me, pulling the toboggan loaded with ice traps, the auger, bait, beer and food. My top thermal has shifted up on the small of my back and I feel the icy metal against my flesh—pale with the indentation of the safety on the pistol.

Jimmy puts a cigarette to his lips and checks his pockets. "You got a light?" he asks, looking back at me. I can't look Jimmy in the eyes. I light his smoke. He turns, and I adjust the gun.

Three days ago, I slept with Jimmy's wife. She pulled me into her softness with her legs, thighs squeezing against my ribs—used her heels to push into the small of my back. Her red hair was tangled in my fingers as I pulled it—hair I smelled while biting the side of her chin. The same hair that sometimes left a hint of its fragrance on Jimmy that I can smell on the wind blowing off his shoulders—sweat and white wine. I've been sleeping with Jimmy's wife for a while—collapsing on top of her on starched hotel sheets with love and guilt swirling in my stomach like the baby she's carrying—my baby.

"We're almost there," I tell Jimmy.

He pushes on. The sliding toboggan whispers against the snow behind him.

The ice shack is fifty yards away. Louie has his snow-mobile parked beside it. Behind the ice shack is the hole. It's the hole exposing water—dark—cold—black, like shadows inside the barrel of a gun. It's the hole we're supposed to dump Jimmy's body in after I kill him.

The snow collects against the seams of my boots and

the straps at the cuffs of my jacket. Cold creeps over my nose across my cheekbones, down the sides of my neck, inside my jacket—curls into a ball against my chest then rolls down my ribs and the insides of my arms—around my wrists where it spins into my palms, between my fingers and over my knuckles like something curious and colorful.

We step up to the door of the ice shack and Louie comes out.

"Hey, Jimmy," he says. He hands him a small pouch with some tools in it. "Take a look at the sled, will ya, Jimmy? It's been stalling out."

Jimmy drops the rope from the toboggan. He looks me in the eyes as he takes the tools. He turns and squats near the engine of the sled. I slip the gun from my pants, click the safety off and hold the muzzle against the back of my leg. Louie takes a step back and moves behind me. I hear his jacket rustling like he's reaching for something. He taps my left shoulder and points at the back of Jimmy's head. Jimmy's breath rolls over his shoulder and I can see the side of his face, the windburn on his cheeks and the snow falling against his neck. I look at Louie and bring the gun up.

I slide the gun across my chest, put the barrel against Louie's jaw and pull the trigger.

The shot blows the hearing out of my left ear. Louie spins and I step away from him. He falls to the snow on his hands and knees, blood spattering from the bottom of his jawless face. Jimmy is crouched on the ice covering his ears. I turn toward Louie, and his babbling howl enters my right ear. Snow is clinging to my eyelashes, making my eyelids quiver to shake them off. I push the barrel against the back of Louie's head.

I pull the trigger again and watch a scarlet burst spray onto his outstretched fingers and the snow. His body collapses. The echo of the gunshot rumbles to the edges of the lake.

Jimmy grabs Louie's feet and I take an arm. We drag him around the ice shack to the hole. When we roll Louie in, water spills out over the ice, making slush out of the snow. Pockets of air bubble inside his jacket, then the faceless body sinks out of sight.

I pull the set of keys from my pocket. There's a red camp on the other side of the lake—a pickup in the driveway. Jimmy takes the keys. He puts them in his pocket.

"You can never come back, Jimmy," I say.

"I know," he says.

"Ice Shack"—Deadfall: Crime Fiction by New England Writers

FISHER OF MEN

The bar at the corner of Highland and Grove smelled like stale death—dried blood and old sweat. Primal urges burst into the air like a Christmas tree on fire. The only window was a murky porthole from a forgotten vessel mounted in the door. The woes and torments of patrons, submerging deeper into their miserably fated descent, lingered inside where they are supposed to be. Others, almost defeated by what they had tried to drink away, would spill into the street only to move forward to a more convenient place of exhaustion. They were all sinners. They were all victims—victims of evolution, the process by which basic survival instincts are replaced with grief, faith or guilt. The bar at the corner of Highland and Grove is where Vanessa Fisher found Ty.

She knew he had perfect vision and didn't go to church. He had no family that he visited or spoke to. He was under six feet tall, handsome. He had a deep voice and a scar on the side of his throat just below his jaw.

She was velvet, a small, elegant creature of capability. She had short blonde hair and eyes the color of broken safety glass. Her smile was sinister, a lunatic grin. She was something that God let fall from the sky with nothing soft to land on—a sinner.

Ty was sitting at the bar, thumbing streaks down the condensation on his glass.

"You want to buy me a shot?" Vanessa asked, tapping his shoulder.

No pushed to his lips, but he said nothing when he looked at her. She sat down. "I like fire," she said.

He smiled. "Preference?"

"Surprise me."

"It'll be the first of many."

"Smooth talker."

Ty ordered the shots.

The flames puffed against the rim of the glass.

She leaned forward, and with a short, solid exhale she extinguished the flame.

Three shots apiece were all they needed. Each time he delivered the shots, the bartender scoured Ty with a glare that promised violence. Then, he would prowl back to the other end of the bar and stare at Vanessa.

They walked the sidewalk. The roots of growing trees had made the cobblestone as uneven and clumsy as their gait. He held her hand, which was tiny and firm, and offered to carry her purse. She refused. Metallic chimes quivered inside it when she pulled it from his reach. It helped her keep her balance, she told him.

She knew nothing of the scar on his neck, that it was a childhood mark of despair—that he'd used a belt to hang himself from the top bunk of his dead brother's bed and when the buckle snapped it cut him. She didn't know he'd had a brother or that he was the reason Ty stopped at the gates of the cemetery each day but never went in.

* * *

There were no pictures in his bedroom, nothing hanging from the walls, no ornamental decorations. He was naked. Hands bound with cotton rope to his headboard. Vanessa pulled a square knot tight and tucked the loose ends gingerly beneath the coils around his ankle. He watched her maneuver the knots with urgent proficiency.

"Where did you learn to tie knots like that?"

She smiled then stuck her tongue between her teeth. "My father."

"He taught you how to tie knots?"

She jerked the last knot tight, rattling the footboard. "He taught me about men."

Straddling him, she kissed hard and wet. Eyes closed, her lips and tongue worked against his like the last, tired thrashings of a netted fish fighting to escape. Ty's neck strained when he chased her tongue as she pulled away.

Vanessa stood and stripped her shirt over her head. He licked his lips to taste. She stepped off the bed and undid her jeans. She kept her back to him and slid them over her ass, down over her legs and off of one foot, then the other.

"I want you to please me." She turned to face him. "Do you want to please me?"

He tried to speak but only nodded. She set the purse on the bed and pulled out a book of matches.

"What are those for?"

"These," she said, placing the matches on his chest, "are for the candles."

She reached back into her purse and pulled out two small glass votives, placed them on the nightstand, then walked to the switch and turned the lights off. She straddled him again. With her wrists together as if they were bound, she pressed her palms against his chest over the matches. Her biceps pressed her breasts to the top of her bra, and he felt an insatiable lust heaving through his torso. His body begged to throw it inside of her—quake the smooth perfection of her skin and voice with gushing tremors and wails. The struck match snapped, jumped wildly into the air then simmered until he could see only her smile. She lit the candles. The flames glowed and cast frantic shadows on the walls.

Vanessa worked him inside of her. She moved her hips in small circles to the beat of her pulse. They whimpered love and promises neither of them could keep—lies to comfort each other until there was no reason to lie anymore. Vanessa collapsed against the clamminess of his chest. Her wet leather moan wrapped around his shoulders. She patted his cheek and kissed the corner of his mouth.

The hand she held on his face slipped to his throat and she ran her thumb down the stiff, brittle scar on his neck.

"Can you guess what people would do if they couldn't have sex?" she asked, slipping her other hand into her purse.

"No."

"They would find interesting ways to kill each other."

Vanessa pulled the knife from her purse. The blade caught glimmers of candlelight. She placed the sharp edge of the steel against his throat below his Adam's apple. His body tensed, and he attempted to pull away. "What are you doing?"

"I'm teaching you about women," she whispered.

Flexing against the ropes only knotted his joints. He was twelve again, trying not to fight for his breath. Trying not to kick, trying to forget his brother chased the ball that he threw. Ty looked, but he could not see her damage. It did not bulge on her flesh, but the wounds were savage and vicious, and no sinner's soul would be saved because of them.

"Fisher of Men"—The Hangover 2010

ECDYSIS

She called him stranger. The only sounds he made were the bristling whispers of his pencil against paper. He burned through sketchbooks drawing only her, compelled by something he could not define even if he'd had the words to do so—something lofty and surreal—the chance to remember a few months of joy in his life before it was over. She forced him to remind himself of why he'd come back.

I came here to find the soul of the boy I was before Miller came. I came back here to forgive him.

James lived in the apartment building owned by Miller, the man who killed his mother. His apartment was on the second floor, across the hall from the barricaded apartment Miller once lived in. There were two bedrooms, one of which was always closed. He had few possessions, none as significant as the scar that dangled just below his collarbone from the bullet of Miller's gun.

He'd returned only for Miller, to end the years of nightmares and feelings of cowardice. He had lived in penance, reliving his boyhood terror, until he saw Kim outside the coffee shop. He'd watched her whimper in her car and press a tissue-wrapped finger to the corners of her eyes. She was the first thing he'd drawn other than Miller, and the sketch was how he'd introduced himself, laying it open on his table in the coffee shop. She gazed at him with a look of confusion when she saw it, an awkwardness that was dismissed by the beauty captured with pencil strokes. It was more than any verbal compliment she had ever received. She lifted the pad from the table, forgetting why she'd been crying.

Only a few days before Miller arrived, it began to rain. Soft drops tapped James' shoulder on his way to see Kim. As he walked into the shop he wondered if her skin tasted like coffee or mocha—if she showered after work and smelled like something other than steamed milk. He brought his cup of coffee to her. She smiled. James pushed his thumbs into the counter while she pressed buttons on the register. Nearly two months had passed, and James maintained the same nervousness despite visiting every day she worked.

"Rain's picking up outside today. You going to stay for a while?"

He nodded.

"Suppose I asked you a question that required more than a yes or no answer."

A shrug.

"Funny, are we? One of these days, stranger."

He sat at a table in the corner and stared at the blank page of the sketchbook. Loneliness surrounds a person when the actions of their past, or lack of action, has made them believe they're a coward. Kim knew nothing of his past. She was patient, unlike paid professionals who sat across from patients and listened to their words like they were someone special. During the moments Kim spent with him, even his silence didn't provoke her to speak of herself. She finished her side cleaning and sat across from him, tapping the jewel case of a CD with her turquoise-painted fingernails. "I think you'll like this. It's loud, like you." She giggled.

Once a week she burned mix CDs of songs she thought he would like. More than anything, she waited for him to speak while her eyes roved over his slanted shoulders, the left noticeably lower than the right. His jaw was wide, his cheeks muscular from years of a stern, unrelenting expression, fibrous as if invisible fingers rolled hard across them. His eyes were different. They were large and hazel, soft and oily, intense and deliberate—a speech all its own radiating a deep, unresolved hurt—agony. She tried not to study him, but her intrigue trumped her manners. He offered that exposure and studied her as well. The way a person's eyes navigate over you, how they move or how their fingers twitch reveal how much they care, or how much they don't. A twitch of the finger can hush a whisper, control the line of a pencil or pull a trigger. He stared at her for a long time, until she looked away and dropped her chin.

"How can you look at me like that and not say anything?"

He broke his stare and set the tip of his pencil against the blank paper and began. It started with her smile, the steam from her cup of coffee which rose past the corner of her mouth to a wave of hair that dropped across her eyebrow. Then her eyes. He penciled in the earrings and shadowed her cheeks—flattened the pencil and formed the bridge of her nose. He drew the scar on her chin last and it didn't come out right. On paper, it looked ugly, like his, but it wasn't ugly, and James couldn't imagine seeing her face without it. He covered the scar by drawing the thumb of a hand resting against her face, his thumb. He tore the finished drawing from the pad and slid it across the table.

And that was the exchange between them, built up over the past several weeks. It was those gestures of compassion that somehow elevated their communication beyond the verbal, as if words would have taken something away from it. There was trust in the absence of his speech. His silence placed him above the disbelief, above the promises that would only be broken—had only ever been broken to her. She took the drawing after brushing her fingertips against his knuckles.

"Do you always draw faces, or is that what you do best?" she asked.

Miller doesn't know my face though he remembers me. He remembers turning to me when I found him, after my mother's screams woke me. She ran through the house followed by his heavy footsteps, and her screaming started again. He was hunched over her when I crept into the kitchen and saw them—my mother lying naked and bloody while Miller stood above her. The knife blurred into a flash of silver with his thrusting. Her eyes stared at me as they went dull in the darkness. I was skinny and trembling, waiting for Miller to use that blade on me.

But he didn't, and I did nothing to save my mother.

Kim took the sketch into the back, where she kept her purse and jacket, then returned to her work. A funeral procession slithered by outside. James finished his coffee and headed home. When he reached the corner, rainwater was rattling gutters and screaming into the storm drains. It was difficult to keep his eyes open through the rain. His clothes were drenched, sucked to the open pores of his skin. He thought of the people at the funeral, if their sorrow gave them a chance to speak of themselves. A car pulled up to the curb, and the driver cracked the passenger window.

"You need a ride, stranger?" Kim asked.

The smells of Kim's car came into the rain weaving through the heavy drops. There was only a short distance left to walk. He wanted to sketch her eyes looking up at him through the small opening of her window—a longing expression that changed to a smile when he got in the car. She palmed the side of his face. Her thumb worked over his eyebrow, and the rainwater trapped there dripped over his cheekbone.

"You'll catch your death in this." Her hand retreated. She gripped the steering wheel and drove. "I have a couple hours of my shift left. Maybe we can go see a movie or something later."

He pulled his look away from her and focused on his hands, the tips of his fingers already pruned and the skin nearly translucent. She pulled the car up to the curb outside his apartment building.

"No? Okay. No problem. I'll see you tomorrow?"

He confirmed with a smile and climbed out of her car, taking one more look at her face.

I saw Miller's face before. I saw his face at the breakfast table before my mother left him. I remember his face in the moonlight. I remember my prone shadow limp against the wall.

The rain cleared sometime in the night while James sketched in the closed bedroom. The music that Kim had given him kept his wrist moving against the paper until the sun crept through the window and up his leg. The sketch on the pad was Miller—his face and James' just over his shoulder. He hadn't drawn Miller in weeks, since he met Kim. When the light had climbed up his body and cast its heat against his cheek, it was time to sleep. He stood and taped the sketch up with the rest of them—a decade worth of nightmares overlapping on the walls like fringe. He centered himself in the room and lay on the floor. Every inch of wall was covered with Miller's face. James worked his eyes around the room, waiting for a few hours of sleep.

He awoke startled by dreams of looking down Miller's barrel again. He moved around the empty rooms of the apartment fading the image in his dream before leaving to see Kim. She met him at the door of the coffee shop. She was not in her uniform. Instead, she wore a lavender tee and khaki shorts which revealed the muscular tone of her thighs. The shirt was tight, form-fitting around her breasts and stomach. Smells of perfume, gardenia and vanilla hand soap. "Forget the coffee today. Come with me." She took his hand and led him to her car. "It's too nice a day to spend it in that coffee shop, and since you won't ask me out, I'm taking you somewhere."

For a moment, while next to Kim, he wanted to speak.

His throat felt like the cloth on the seat of an old junk car—dry and stiff. He wanted to break the dryness, crack away the stiffness and come back to life. Kim remained silent. The place she took him was an evergreen forest dissected by a gravel road. The trees were slim and had been intentionally planted to form a grid. She stopped at the base of the hill, where there was a large log preventing farther travel. "I come here when I want quiet." She pulled an ice cube from the cup in her console and put it in her mouth.

Outside, the air smelled of pine, and James immediately forgot the bland smell of concrete and sand and stale water that he was accustomed to. She pulled a blanket from the trunk of her car, a pad and a package of pencils. They were good paper and charcoal pencils, unlike the number twos he used. James squinted his eyes at them and clenched his jaw. Kim's smile disappeared. "You like to sketch. I thought maybe you would like to use something a little more professional." She looked for her smile somewhere on the ground, as if she'd dropped it there. He slipped the pad and pencils from her fingers, feeling their bony slenderness and the cool smoothness of her fingernails. His eyes went slick looking at the gifts in his hands.

Blue jays fluttered from the branches above them and screeched as they flew ahead. He followed her to a clearing in the pines where there was a patch of grass and three headstones leaning forward toward their sunken graves. American flags were pinned into the ground beside them from Memorial Day. Kim spread the blanket, draping it over the grass and stray pine needles. Her hamstrings went taut and the muscles of her calves flexed and relaxed like flashes of lightning. She lay on her side and spotted her head with her hand, so her wrist was facing him. Her other arm was folded over her stomach as she pulled tiny balls of wool from the blanket. He sat on the edge of the blanket and drew so that the contour of her body faded into the tombstones behind her. Between the pushes of each breeze, which grew stronger and more frequent, he could hear her breathing. Her lips were parted slightly, glistening from the wetness of the melting ice in her mouth, and strands of her hair tickled her nose as it hung between her eyes. He crested each line on the paper in the way he wanted to run his palm over her body—her lips, the way he wanted to brush his own lips against her.

When the sketch was finished, she took the pad and rubbed the tips of her fingers over the paper. "Is this a personal choice of yours, to be silent?"

He nodded.

"And you never use sign language?"

He shook his head.

"How do you communicate?"

The sky had darkened, and a threatening purr of thunder came from the distance. He lifted the strands of hair from her nose, curled them behind her ear and leaned toward her. Her tongue was still cold from the ice cube. The kiss was brief, a one-syllable whisper against her lips. He withdrew, and she left her mouth partway open, expecting more. Around them, single blades of grass twitched in response to drops of rain. Her fingers crawled over his neck and she flattened out on her back, pulling him to her.

Her teeth chattered on the way home. The rain had dropped on them in a single, sudden burst, chasing them from the forest like critters of nuisance. The sheen of rainwater on her legs and arms quivered James' heartbeat and breathing into a frenzied shudder unmatched by what he would feel later, before he spoke to her.

In his apartment, Kim stood shivering in his living room, taking in the simplicity of his place. He'd hung only a few sketches on the walls of his living room, all of her, and all a far more attractive perspective than what she believed she actually was. She wondered, as she wondered what his voice sounded like, what else he had drawn.

James came from the bathroom and handed her a towel. She dried her face and the back of her neck, then started on her arms. "No possessions. Stoic vow of silence. You a monk?"

He smiled.

Kim left the next morning, before Miller arrived to collect the rent. James thought of Kim's lips against his, how her fingers circled the scar on his chest. He sat on the edge of his bed and unfolded a newspaper clipping. The paper had yellowed, but the words were still clear. Words he knew by heart. James lifted the mattress and took one of the pistols there. He carried it and the newspaper clipping into the apartment across the hall. The plywood sheet covering the door pulled easily from the doorframe. He pushed it to the side and entered the empty apartment where he taped the obituary to the wall left of the door. On the other side of the room, where there was a mantle, James placed the gun.

Miller began his monthly sweep through the building. James waited by his door, touching his neck where Kim pressed her lips before she'd left. Miller made his way to the second floor. Kim's whisper echoed in James' mind, the word she said while her arms wrapped around his back and her fingers pulled against his skin. *Speak*. All he had to give was the sound of his voice but giving that to her would take away the certainty of what he needed for Miller.

Miller stopped at the empty apartment. His footsteps were muted as he moved inside. James entered the apartment and stood just inside the doorway. Miller's envelopes of rent money were scattered at his feet. He lifted the corner of the obituary with his index finger and James wondered if he'd ever read it. For a long time, his mother's screams had been wails begging him to join her.

Miller turned unflinching.

James put his hands behind his back and guided Miller to the mantle with a glance. Miller's eyes were thin and dark, overshadowed by thick eyebrows and shaggy hair. He moved slowly, a lip twitching at the corner of his mouth, the stranger's face fading into the child's that Miller remembered. James' hands were still, and his body relaxed as Miller reached for the gun. He pulled the slide back slightly to check for a chambered round, then looked at James wondering what he had expected him to do—use the gun on himself?

Miller pointed the gun at him and shot. A sudden weightlessness came over James' body as if he'd finally torn through the shadow of the boy in the hallway. There was only sound—a vacuous threat—words without passion.

Powder residue. It needed to be on Miller's hands or it wouldn't look right. James had removed the bullet and, instead, stuffed tissue into the casing. He snapped the pistol from his back pocket and closed the distance between himself and Miller with two quick steps. Miller's lips parted, maybe to curse him, maybe to beg, but James pressed the gun to Miller's lips before he could do either. Miller's breath whistled against the barrel. James flexed his finger. The slide pumped back and settled—a twitch in his hand as if he'd broken the point of a pencil.

"Ecdysis"—Rose & Thorn Journal Spring 2010

GRIP

Bare branches clawed at the sky and revealed the church steeple in the distance. Emily Grant made her way out of the woods toward the landmark. She kicked through the wet leaves on the ground. The red-yellow rust color tourists took pictures of, colors that rested flat and glossy in calendars for people who lived below, where the black and white bars contained their days, had been brought down by the rain. Leaves clung to the bottom of her right sock. The pink, untied laces of her left sneaker dragged over wet tar.

Slices on her bare shins burned where the brambles tangled her legs and feet—how she'd lost her shoe. She crossed the road, all by herself, a secret she told herself to keep so her parents wouldn't get angry. She tried to walk faster but the cut just above her knee stung when she bent her leg too much. She should have crawled under that barbed wire fence.

Emily could smell the moss and soil on the back of her hands when she wiped her tears. She smeared a dark streak over her small, freckled nose. Her hair pulled against her scalp, matted and tangled. She saw the corner where the bus dropped her off from school, where she'd dropped her art project the day before and the wind took it away. Her stomach tightened, and she wished she hadn't given her snack to the Winslow boy who never had a snack and sometimes wore the same shirt two days in a row, just like she did today. She wondered if the kids would laugh at her, too.

Blood had dried to her cheek from where the glass cut her during the crash. Her tongue was dry, and she wanted something to drink. She wished she could taste something other than metal and leather, what his hand tasted like when he put it over her mouth. Emily wondered about cavities because she didn't brush before she fell asleep out there in the woods. She wondered if her mother would be mad that she hadn't been wearing her safety belt.

Emily hobbled faster, despite the pain from the cut on her leg. She fell to her knees on her front lawn and let the wet grass soothe the burning against her shins. She sprawled out so the coolness would seep into her thighs and ease the cramping that had come after she ran from the crash. Then she heard footsteps. A voice yelled that they got her.

The front door opened. Her mother peeled around the men exiting. The woman's grip was tighter than the man who'd put her in the car. Emily nestled her face against the fabric of her mother's blue cashmere sweater. Warmth fell on the back of her neck when they passed into the house. She looked toward the calendar hanging beside the door. All the days up to yesterday had been crossed off, that single black and white space that the rest of her life would cling to.

CIRCUMFERENCE

Close to midnight, the bus rushed down a lightless highway and Mae Vaughn strained to see past her reflection into the darkness outside, but she couldn't. Pale blue eyes and everything about her were as sharp as the blade she was holding. The flame she held to the blade, though, was soft and round. She sat in the last seat on the bus near the lavatory. There were three other passengers, all succumbing to the rocking as the vehicle groaned along and they fell into their own comfortable slumbers, dreaming of what they'd left behind or what they were headed to. Mae Vaughn glanced up to the driver, who sipped his coffee. She put the lighter on the seat and pulled the belt-line of her jeans down. She squeezed the strap of her purse tight between her teeth and whimpered when she put the blade to the name tattooed on the soft flesh along the ridge of her hip—Kensey Waite.

The assumption of metal and cement is that they can keep a man contained so they combine the two to build prisons, yet all they contain is cold, even when the sun beams through the barred windows. Kensey could always find relief in the coldness of the walls on his bare back or against his forehead when he leaned into the bars as he waited. The seasons rolled and tumbled over each other like young playful pets until Kensey walked out of the prison to the car waiting for him.

Kensey kicked the mud from his shoes and reached for the pack of cigarettes on the dashboard before slumping into the passenger seat. He waved his fingers near the lighter, anticipating the click and bounce. Tank watched them, mesmerized almost, by the blackened thumbnail, the lightning bolts on the web of his hand below his thumb, and the wedding band he wore on his index finger. Kensey took a long drag and trapped a cough in his throat behind clenched teeth.

"Go," he said.

Tank pulled the shifter down one gear too many, readjusted, and the car moved forward with mud and water lapping and slurping at the tires. Tank rubbed his stomach then pulled on the flap of his jacket. His body odor drifted over to Kensey, who ignored it except to roll his window down and lean closer to the air blowing in.

"You want food?" Tank asked.

"Nah."

"You mind if I stop and get a slice?"

Kensey looked at his stomach and the flesh revealed below his shirt. "Wouldn't want you to go hungry."

At the store, Kensey stood outside with a fresh cigarette and leaned against the front fender. Tank went in, and Kensey watched children riding in circles on their bicycles, skirting the edges of puddles with a dotted spray of brown up the back of their shirts. He finished his cigarette and flicked it into a footprint in the mud. Twenty minutes later, Tank came out with a pizza box and his hand under the lid pulling out a slice.

Tank slipped into the seat and maneuvered the box into the vehicle, stretching his head back to pull the pizza in between his neck and above the steering wheel. He slid the box on the dash. Tank was slipping a crust back into the box and reaching for another slice when Kensey swung himself into the back seat.

"What are you doing?" Tank asked, adjusting the rear-view to see Kensey.

"Like old times," he responded, looking away from Tank's opened mouth chewing. "Let's ride around awhile. I'd like to see what's changed since I've been gone."

Tank shifted the car into gear with his left hand. They pulled onto Congress Street and drove toward the West End, past Monument Square, where the schizophrenics wailed and screamed at passing cars. Dreadlocked hippies strummed chords on out-of-tune guitars with the cases open, and the few dimes and crumpled bills in there waited for more to arrive. The panhandlers who were jaundiced and dirty moaned their mantra, spare change, and expelled the stench of beer into the wind. The car stopped at a red light. Tank began his fourth slice. The corner at the library was fenced off for renovations. They moved on, up the hill past the chain stores and bars where the hipsters wore their black skinny jeans and smoked hand-rolled cigarettes with PBR pounders held between their knees. Continuing, they passed the hotel, its plaza swarming with pigeons and gulls diving for thrown cheese doodles and bread. Bums napped on benches, moving occasionally to wave the flies away. At Longfellow Square, Tank turned left and quickly right, passing the adult toy store and the fag bar. When they reached the promenade, Tank had finished half the pizza.

Kensey made his way to a nearby bench, extended his arms across the backrest and stared blankly through the budding trees toward the oil tanks and the Route 1 Bridge. Tank carried the pizza box from the car and took a seat next to Kensey.

"What are you going to do about Mae?"

"You know where she is?"

"I tracked her to Buffalo, then Chicago. She stayed in San Francisco for a year. She's up in Toronto now."

"Maybe she thinks because I'm not supposed to leave the country I won't."

"I think you should leave the area. When the Somalis find out you've been released, they're going to—"

"What makes you think they don't already know?"

Tank stopped chewing and lowered his slice of pizza down to the box resting on his lap. "You should get out of here then. I have a place down in Florida you could stay."

"I'm not going anywhere."

"Where did you hide the money?"

"In a place where no one goes."

Tank thought for a moment. "I still can't believe she did it, Kensey."

"Sending me to prison kept me safer than being on the street."

"The Brotherhood?"

Kensey nodded.

In the car, Kensey unfolded a slip of paper he'd pulled from his pocket and read the address to Tank. They drove down Forrest Avenue into Westbrook to the address. Tank parked the car across the street and looked at Kensey.

"This is a halfway house."

Kensey nodded and tapped a cigarette from his pack.

They waited for hours, watching the work bus drop off parolees. The streetlights came on dimly and grew brighter as the sunlight faded and night arrived. Kensey burned through his pack of cigarettes, and Tank fought his curiosity to ask why they were there. They watched a group of smokers stand beneath the streetlight. Kensey took no particular interest in any of them until one man came out of the house to join the group. The other men stopped laughing and talking, flicked their cigarettes and went back into the house leaving the man to smoke alone. Kensey leaned forward and folded his arms over the dashboard.

"He's popular," Tank said. "You know that guy?"

"Ratted on my cellmate. Fucker got done indecent because of him."

"What are you going to do?"

"I might cut his head off."

Mae Vaughn's telephone rang while she flattened her hair in the laundry room with an iron. It was long, and she had dyed it black. A gray cat rolled to his back and stretched his legs on the sofa when she passed.

"Hello?"

"Ms. Waite?"

"Who is this?"

"This is Detective Robertson. I'm calling to inform you that your husband was released from prison an hour ago. If you'd—"

Mae hung up the phone and ran to the door. She checked

the deadbolt and, despite her apartment being on the fifth floor, she went around the house to check the windows. The cat leapt to the table and stroked his paw with his tongue then rolled it over his right ear. The phone began ringing again. She charged at it and pulled the cord from the wall.

Tank set a bottle of Senator's Club whiskey on the table. Kensey, shirtless and skinnier than Tank remembered, twisted the plastic top from the bottle and took a long, burning pull. He shook his head and took another.

"What are you doing?"

"Getting drunk," Kensey answered.

"Do you want some coke or something?"

"Snort or soda?"

"Soda."

"No. Did you get the sander?"

Tank nodded and pulled a palm sander from a paper bag. "What's this for?"

Kensey gulped another pull and looked down at the iron cross tattooed on his ribs, just below his left pec. The ink was faded and green. Below his other pec was a clock with no hands. Kensey ripped another two gulps from the bottle.

"Did you bring the other stuff?" Kensey asked, stretching the sander cord to an outlet.

"Yeah, but you're not going to do what I think you are, are you?"

"No. You are."

Tank wiped his palms over the flaps of his shirt. "Nah, nah, nah. I can't do that, Kensey."

Kensey pulled the revolver Tank had left for him from his back pocket. He pulled the hammer back and pointed it at Tank's stomach. "I'll shoot you right in your fucking gut."

A look of hurt rolled over Tank's face.

"Aw, you gonna cry, fat-fuck. Cry for me. Let me see those big, whimpering, fat-boy tears. C'mon Tank."

Tank maintained his look while Kensey took a pull from the bottle and blamed his watering eyes on the harshness of the whiskey. He slid the hammer forward, stood and swatted Tank's cheek with the gun.

"Pick up the sander or I will fuck you up."

Kensey sat and lifted his left hand to the top of his head. Tank picked up the sander, stepped toward Kensey and thumbed the switch.

The humming of the hand tool made Kensey's skin tingle until Tank pressed the rounded edge into the center of his tattoo. It was a quick, bike-dumping, road-rash kind of burn until the first several layers of skin were gone and Kensey's blood slid over the grit of the sandpaper. The pain settled into the bone, vibrating ribs, and sent a twisting pain through Kensey's neck. Tank worked the machine up and down, and the pain became a source of lucid memories for Kensey—memories pulled to help him through the pain— the way Mae's cheeks drained pale when she caught a glimpse of him from the stand at his trial, the last he'd seen of her face. As he looked up at Tank's face, he saw that the words he'd used had fallen like timber against the back of the only friend he had.

When it was done, and Kensey felt the coolness of his blood sliding along the groove of his hip, the two men sat across from each other at the table. Tank pulled in wheezing breaths over his bottom lip. His chin and red cheeks were freckled with drying blood. Kensey sat hunched over with his left shoulder and the wound facing Tank. He lit a cigarette and tossed the lighter onto the table. The bottle of Senator's Club was half empty.

Kensey lifted his head. "I'm sorry, Tank. I didn't mean those things."

Tank stood. "Your car is in the garage." He tossed a set of keys on the table and left.

Mae Vaughn lay in bed, running her finger over the scar that had once been a mark of slightly raised, inked skin in the form of Kensey's name. She'd eliminated every reminder of him: the tattoo, pictures, even little phrases of his she'd adopted into her own vernacular. The cat, even, which was crunching away on food at his dish, she'd taken in because Kensey was allergic. She tried to remember his face—the face that would come for her. She'd spent years pressing her lips against that face, waking to it, brushing sweat from it. The last time she'd seen it before she testified against him, she'd slapped it. But she couldn't remember it. She remembered his smell. Even after five years had passed, sometimes her dreams would trick her into smelling him in the room, on her sheets, biting gently into her shoulder. Each day had been longer than she wanted to endure, but five years had passed, and yesterday, it seemed, she gave herself the scar she was rubbing.

Tank found a bar that was mostly empty and sulked in a corner with a plate of nachos and a gin and tonic. Halfway through his drink he hadn't touched his nachos, and the gin was giving him heartburn. The weight against his leg was gaining. In the bathroom, he unraveled the bottom of the bag of shit clinging to the adhesive around his stoma and emptied it into the toilet—a daily reminder of the 12-gauge round that should have killed him.

When Tank returned to the house, Kensey's car was gone. The floor and table had been cleaned of the sprays and spots of blood. The neck of the whiskey bottle was broken off. The cord of the palm sander was wrapped tightly around the neck of the man sprawled out on the kitchen floor. The yellowed white of his dull eyes bulged from his head. The crude-oil darkness of his skin seemed impossible to Tank, and his hopes of ever seeing Kensey alive again vanished.

The Somalis brought one-million-and-a-half dollars' worth of heroin into the Portland Harbor every two weeks, which is why every two weeks it was practically impossible to get a cab on a Friday night. Somalis took control of the livery industry with the influx of refugees. They stacked themselves in apartments, collected a government check and saved enough to buy a car. Half of them didn't have licenses, but as long as the cab was stickered, there was no reason for the cops to pull them over without bearing the stigma of racial profiling. From the harbor, they transported the product to places like South Portland, Lewiston, Sanford and Biddeford for the big deals. The rest they peddled out of their cabs. Kensey tracked it all up from that—one low-level dealer passing a bundle.

The night of a drop-off, Kensey and Tank called a cab.

They waited for the dented Lincoln to pull up to the curb. Tank climbed in the back seat. Kensey went around the car and rapped on the driver's window.

"You speak English?"

"Yes, good," the cabbie answered.

The cabbie pressed the fare button on his meter. "Where you are going?"

"Which way is east?" Tank asked.

"Excuse please?" The cabbie looked back at Tank. Kensey slipped a zip tie around the door frame and the opening in the driver's window. Tank lifted the sawed-off and rested it on the seat.

"In case you want to pray," Kensey said, climbing into the cab.

"Nononononononono." The cabbie looked away from the gun and held his hands up. He glanced at Kensey in the rearview and turned again toward the barrel of Tank's shotgun. "You Mr. Kensey. I see you in the papers. Mr. Kensey, why you do this to me?"

"Asa lama lakum, motherfucker. We're going to your drop tonight. You don't get out of this cab before your brains do unless you do everything I tell you to. Now drive."

The cabbie fidgeted and tried to regain his composure. He pulled the cab awkwardly back onto the street.

"Don't forget to call in," Kensey whispered.

The cabbie pressed his two-way against his lips. "Pickup, number seven."

Ten-four.

"We should bail," Tank told Kensey. Kensey refused. The cabbie already knew his name. The consequences would be the same. Kensey made the cabbie drive to an empty school parking lot and kill the cab light. "You're done for the night. Call it in."

The cabbie maneuvered more calmly that time. "Clear. Number seven out of seat."

Ten-four.

When the time came, Kensey explained to the driver to make his pick-up. They dropped Tank off on the corner of Commercial and India, where Mae sat waiting and hotboxing her cigarettes. Before the cabbie drove down to the wharf, Kensey put a .45 hollow point piece of lead, mushroomed out from impact, in the cabbie's hand. "That's what a bullet looks like after it penetrates skull." Then Kensey sunk to the floor and pulled a blanket over him.

After the pick-up, Mae and Tank followed the cab to Biddeford where it pulled into the parking lot of an apartment building. Behind every window flashed the silhouette of a pit bull or Rottweiler. The cabbie pressed the button in the glove box to pop the trunk and moments later, Kensey watched it open and close. There were two men. One of them rapped on the hood and their footsteps stopped.

"What the fuck is that?" One of the men asked, rubbing his fingers over the flange of the zip tie.

"Yo, what the fuck is—"

The other man pulled on the handle. Kensey dumped three rounds into the door. The men scrambled on the ice, shooting wildly at the cab, clipping the cabbie. The cabbie gassed it toward the exit. When he took the turn, Kensey flew from the back seat out onto the snow as he tried to pull himself up by the door handle. The stairway to the apartment filled with shirtless and T-shirted men. Kensey emptied his clip, forcing the men to spill down the stairs and over the railing or duck back into the apartment.

Mae's car slid sideways into the parking lot, bumping the rear fender of the cab just enough to push the Lincoln out of control and into a snow bank. Tank swung from the car and blasted both barrels of his shotgun at the stairwell.

Kensey slipped a fresh clip into his pistol and shot the lock on the trunk of the cab. He kicked the trunk open and slung the bag of cash inside over his shoulder.

"East is behind you," he told the cabbie who was sprawled over the seat, pawing at the gunshot wound in his leg.

It seemed like it had happened only moments before. Tank went outside and took a moment to study the neighbors' windows. He went back into the house and pulled the gas line from the stove. Under the sink, he found a box of steel wool, put it in the microwave and cranked the dial. Tank hurried from the house, dropping the dead man's wallet in the empty flower bed outside the door.

Mae was making her way through Maine from Canada to Emden Pond. She traveled down route 201, the path that Benedict Arnold used to help defeat the French in the war—a forgotten, failed endeavor. She and Kensey had spent their honeymoon on the pond at the lake house Kensey had stayed during the summers when he was a kid. They'd planned their life together there—dreams, hopes and children. At night, they had lain outside on the dock, staring into the sky—naked, huddled close against the crisp breeze off the water. Kensey'd slid her wedding band up and down her finger. "No matter what happens," he'd said, "we'll always come full circle."

* * *

The detectives brought Tank into the morgue, smiling and joking with one another. The room was exactly how Tank had imagined it—tile walls, lots of shiny metal. Bright. Too bright. He couldn't help but be saddened by the fact that he had actually foreseen all of it.

The body lay beneath the sheet with nothing but ruffles where Kensey's head should have been. That, he hadn't imagined. Even knowing the brutality of the crime, the body looked fake, twisted and awkward from being in the trunk of Kensey's car—a sick joke laid out before him. They pulled the sheet to the waistline, exposing the chest and the wound below his pec. The clock tattoo seemed smaller and more faded. Tank glanced over the body at the shoulders, then elbows. He looked away at the sight of the wrists.

"Is it him? Is this Kensey Waite?"

By the water, Mae listened to the loons howling across the stillness—flat, black, and a perfect reflection of the sky and moon. In front of the house, she pulled a pallet from an old well and reached down to the piece of rebar sticking out of the cement. She worked the knot loose from the metal and pulled the bag from the depth of the well.

In the next town over, Mae stopped at the Solon Hotel and ordered a scotch on the rocks. The man next to her slid his empty beer bottle to the edge of the bar and focused on the news.

A body discovered five days ago in the trunk of a vehicle in a Portland parking garage has been identified as thirty-

seven-year-old Kensey Waite. Six years ago, Waite was found guilty of aggravated assault with a deadly weapon for shooting a Portland cab driver. Waite's wife testified for the prosecution in his trial to which Waite received five years in Warren State Prison. His wife was not available for comment.

"Sounds to me like she deserved to die that way," the man said.

The news slid into its feel-good story about pet adoption. Mae lifted the drink to her lips, ice rattling against the glass from her trembling hands. She took the scotch in one swallow, paid for her drink and went to the restroom. Her eyes watered, but she did the best she could to put on her makeup—mascara and lipstick. She gave up on the eyeliner. A few strands of hair clung to her black dress. She pulled them away and twisted them from her fingers into the sink. Outside the bar, she took a deep breath and clenched her hands together. She hadn't been that nervous since her wedding day.

Her car idled in the parking lot and Mae squinted tears from her eyes. They rolled to her lips where she smoothed them away with her tongue. She didn't see his hand until it was against her face. His blackened thumbnail slid along the edge of her jaw and her breathing slowed.

"Did you miss me, Kensey?" she asked.

Kensey moved forward in the back seat. His breath tickled her ear. "I told you we'd come full circle."

Mae smiled and pushed her cheek into his palm.

"Circumference"—Thuglit May/June 2010

CLOSER

The frays of blood vessels broke his eyes into jagged, yellow-white fragments. Through the tightened skin on the old man's face, his eyes bulged, and Audrey thought that at any moment any jarring, or even a sneeze, would force them to shatter like the bones in the boy he had killed. It was almost winter, a season she loved because even in the cold pages of the books she surrounded herself with, she found warmth on Maine winter nights. But, in those eyes that stared back at her impatiently, she felt a chill writhe through her bones.

Hobbs, the old man, was small. His shoulders drooped, and he breathed heavily as if the walk from the shelves to the front desk with the one book was a lifetime of work. He was an old man when she'd seen him last, when she was a girl. Hobbs muffled a hack in his throat. He smelled of sweat and dirt and wet ashtrays. His short index fingers tapped the edge of the book, waiting for her to scan the barcode and his card.

"I'd like to read this before I turn to dust."

The other librarians snickered behind her. She'd been

holding the heavy, metal scanning pen like a dagger and she quickly relaxed her hand. She dragged the tip of the device across his card and then over the barcode on the back of the book. He took the book without another word, and the librarians watched him shamble through the exit.

Audrey excused herself to the other women and went to the ladies' room. She wanted to be away from the smell he left in the air—the smell that man had carried on the day he killed her little brother Jack. She remembered Jack stepping from the sidewalk to reach for a penny in the gutter on their way to the park. Then Jack was gone, like some prehistoric beast had gobbled him up, leaving a small Velcro shoe propped against the sidewalk. He had been so close it didn't seem real. She heard the sirens and the quiet voices of people gathering at the edges of the sidewalk. The whine and chug of Hobbs' truck engine and the skipping beats of her own heart. Hobbs shuffled to his truck after he'd assessed the damage. He returned with a paper sack, the open neck of a bottle poking out. The police arrived first, and when they approached Hobbs, he lifted the bottle and gulped down whatever was inside of it. When he took the bottle from his lips, he smirked at his own delightful cleverness.

She wondered how many days she'd thought of her little brother while that man shuffled through the library—that smirk he wore on his face when the prosecution couldn't prove he was drunk when he'd hit Jack, and the jury convicted him of negligent homicide. For years, she'd harbored some relief in the hope the man had died, but no. All the pain he had caused her had never been redeemed—Hobbs moved through the world, wafting his miserable odor into the faces of the people he made to suffer. She squeezed the

porcelain of the sink until cramps invaded the space between the bones of her hands. When she left the bathroom,
she could still smell him, heavy in the air like something
dead and rotten in the wall. The rest of the day she grew
anxious to be home, in her bed after a long bath, to have
Chance close to her.

When Chance got home from work, Audrey was in bed
propped against the headboard with the faint light from
the table lamp on the nightstand lighting the pages of a
book of poetry. All the poetry she read was in French,
undiluted, she'd told him once, by translation. The room
smelled of vanilla, the candles she'd lit on the dresser. The
edges of her lips were burgundy from the wine she'd been
drinking—nothing but swill left in the stemless glass and a
few drops left in the bottle. He sat down on the ottoman
at the foot of her bed and looked at her in the mirror.

"Rough day?" he asked her reflection. He pulled his
shirt over his head and leaned over his knees to untie his
boots. The scars on his back between his ribs from shivs
and other makeshift prison weapons warped and slipped
closer to his stomach.

"I saw him today."

"Who?"

"The man who killed Jack."

"Oh." He turned to face her. "Are you okay?"

Audrey closed her book and put it on the pillow beside
her. "I'll be fine."

"Talk about it?"

"No." She pulled the comforter tighter around her waist.

Chance turned back to the mirror and toed his boots

from his heels, letting them thump on the floor.

"What's it like to kill a man?" she asked.

He rubbed his palms over his face. "We've talked about that."

"I know. I'm sorry. I'm drunk. I don't really know why I asked. I guess I just wanted to know."

She pulled the comforter off her legs and crawled to the end of the bed. She wrapped her arms around his shoulders and nuzzled into his neck, taking in a deep breath, the scent of sawdust and sweat—the musk of his labor.

"I need a shower, babe. Join me?"

"I took a bath earlier. Hurry and come lie down with me for a while."

She let her arms fall from his shoulders and lay against her pillows to wait for him.

The next day at the library, Audrey shelved books in the mystery section while the other women sipped on their coffee and talked about their book club meeting the night before. When Audrey first started at the library, her first summer out of college, she devoured fiction. It was a relief to be able to lose herself in a story and not the dull monotone of nonfiction and critical assessment. Audrey found comfort in the agenda of their characters, how simple they made primal desire seem with the most complex of motives. Sex and murder were about taking control—easing the searing burn placed against the soul like the blue flame of an acetylene torch. She enjoyed the older novels best, the hardboiled stuff. The newer novels about gunshot residue and microfibers—the elimination of hardboiled detectives replaced by dorky lab rats with clean white robes and delicate fingers killed her interest in the genre.

When Wendy and the other girls went to get their lunch, Audrey pulled Hobbs' information up on the computer. She stopped herself from writing the information down, deciding it was a bad idea for one reason or another. She scoured through the information and repeated the address to herself. When the girls returned, she went about her day filing books, organizing the magazine and periodical racks.

At the end of the day she drove to Acton. The address Hobbs had on file brought her to a large garage on Route 109. There was a camper beside the garage, unlevel on a flat tire, and the roof was covered with a blue tarp. There was a picnic table in front of the camper that Hobbs lay over. A half-empty bottle was cradled in the crook of his elbow. Just past the garage was a small dirt road that she pulled onto and stopped her car, unseen from the road. A wind flexed through the trees, scattering dead leaves, and the smell of Hobbs came to her.

Audrey drove to the Kittery Trading Post and made her way through the clothing and camping sections to the upstairs where they sold guns. She walked along the glass display, admiring the difference in elegance and the brutishness of weapons. The first person to help her was a man in his mid-twenties. His round face and the scatter of facial hair made him seem much younger, boyish. In fact, she could only see him as a boy in her mind. She stopped over a rack of small revolvers, clutching the straps of her purse and keeping it tucked closely to her body with her elbow.

"Can I help you find something?" he asked.

"I don't know. I don't know very much about guns."

"I do. My dad and I have forty-three altogether. Seventeen of those are handguns."

"That's a lot."

"Yeah. You can never have too many guns. So, what are you interested in a gun for? Personal protection? Target shooting?"

"Personal protection, I suppose."

"I carry a forty-five in my truck. Most people nowadays think a 9mm is the way to go, but that won't stop shit. I even put a laser sight on it, too, and a hi-cap magazine."

"A laser sight?"

"Yeah. It shoots a red laser out and wherever you see a red dot is where your bullet is going. You know, like the movies."

"Oh. And what's a hi-cap magazine?" She felt she should be writing things down. And she felt foolish, discouraged she hadn't done any research before she went there. She even began to wonder why she'd driven there in the first place. Surely there were places closer to her home that she could have bought a gun.

"High capacity. A hi-cap magazine is just like a regular magazine except it holds more rounds. A regular clip, that's a magazine, will hold about ten rounds, but with a hi-cap it holds about fourteen."

"Why so many bullets?"

"Well, you know, just in case you miss your target."

"But what about the laser sight?"

The boy pushed his hands in his pockets and craned his head back. He began to move his chin from side to side in bewilderment or annoyance, she couldn't tell. Before he had a chance to respond, another man approached and asked the boy to help in a different section of the store.

When the boy left, she waited for the older man to speak. "What kind of gun are you looking for, dear?" He was less enthusiastic when he asked her, which made her feel more comfortable though she didn't know why.

"Personal protection. We got about that far." She waved her finger from her chest to the boy who had helped her. "I don't know anything about these things, really."

"You know they're not toys, right?"

"Yes, sir. In all honesty, they scare me."

"Well, that's good. That means you'll respect them. If you're looking for personal protection…" He motioned her to follow him down to another display case—the revolvers that she had initially found. He unlocked the sliding glass door behind the case and pulled out a snub-nose revolver. "…this little beauty is probably going to be the best option for you." He checked the round cylinder and the barrel and handed it to her. She placed her purse on the glass and took the gun from him. It was heavier than she'd anticipated, and it seemed anxious to do harm, but there was a comfort about it that she admired. It reminded her of Chance.

"Now, that is a .357 magnum. It's hammerless with a two-inch barrel and it will hold five rounds. I recommend this to all female customers looking for a weapon for personal protection because you can shoot it from your pocket or your purse and you don't have to worry about the hammer getting caught on anything."

"I'll take it."

"That was easy. I'll need to see your driver's license."

The man gave her a form to fill out. She paused over some of the questions, because of Chance, but finished the paperwork and waited for the man to make his phone call.

When the phone call was over, and after the man had run her credit card, he handed her the weapon in a box and two boxes of ammunition. Before he let go of it, he told her, "Make sure you have someone teach you about handling and shooting this. I'd highly recommend a handgun safety course. There are two types of rounds there. The .38's you can use to practice with, and the .357's you should use for protection. I hope it never comes to that." She smiled and kept smiling until she got into her car. She rested the box on the passenger seat, and it was then that she realized, not that she had forgotten exactly, why she had bought the gun. She became conscious of the events that were now in motion, and a brief panic came over her as if she had already committed the crime. For the first time in her life, as many times as she tried to think of something other than the day she wailed over the crumpled body of her brother, she forced herself to think of it—his small body heaped in a sack of tattered bloody clothes and Hobbs leaning against the bed of his truck, gazing around at every-thing but what he'd done.

She waited at the kitchen table for Chance to come home, and in the time that she waited she brushed her fingers over the steel. Like Chance, the gun looked brutal. But she knew that brutality would protect her as much as it could hurt her—the gamble women suffer every day, she thought. When she met Chance, it was in the library. He was look-ing for a book he said wasn't in his other library. She found out later that he was referring to the prison library where he'd been for three years. The official charge was manslaughter, but Wendy had told her murder. Chance walked with his elbows close to his body; he moved fluidly. When he spoke to her, he kept his gaze over her shoulders or at the windows for their reflection of what stood behind him. She led him to the fiction section and pulled a copy of *Desolation Angels* from the shelf.

"Let me know if you need help finding anything else," she told him.

"I don't have a card."

"That's not a problem. Just as long as you have your ID. I'll get you set up when you're ready to check out."

He'd simply nodded to her while cradling the book in his hands.

When Chance approached the front desk, Audrey listened to Wendy stir and whisper to the other librarians. Chance smiled to Audrey and gave her his ID. Before she could fill in Chance's information, Wendy had stepped beside her and she spoke. "I'm sorry, but we're no longer offering cards."

"I don't understand," Chance said.

"We've reached our quota for the month. I'm sorry, sir."

"I see." He held his hand out for Audrey to return his ID. She handed it back to him, confused and embarrassed, hoping Wendy would explain further which she did only after Chance had left.

After work that day, Audrey hurried home and took her copy of the book from her shelf. She drove to the address she'd remembered from Chance's ID. He came to the door of the apartment and stood expressionless behind the screen. She fumbled for something to say, realizing her impulsivity then, and she wondered how foolish he thought she was.

"I'm sorry about what happened today, at the library," she finally said. "Wendy is a—"

"Cunt."

She pursed her lips and nodded. He opened the door and stepped outside. She gripped the book tighter.

"Anyway, I brought this for you." She handed him the book, but he kept his arms at his side.

"Why?"

"I felt bad, and I don't know. This is stupid. I'm sorry."

"Wait." Chance extended his arm and caught her wrist with the tips of his fingers as she turned. His grip was gentle with the firm immediacy of a child's. "Thank you. It's very sweet, but you don't know me. It's pretty dangerous to do what you've done—come to a stranger's house like this."

"I wasn't really thinking."

"No shit. You do this often?"

"Only when I want to get laid," she laughed desperately, again realizing she'd probably said the wrong thing. "Sorry. I was joking."

"You're funny. You want to come in? I'll keep in mind that you're joking about the getting laid thing."

She sat with Chance in his small apartment for hours talking about the books that he'd read. She suggested books to him and laughed at the books he'd been reluctant to read but did so because there were no other choices. He offered her an explanation to his crime before she could ask. And when he explained it, she found a comfort in his honesty despite the facts of his confession—that it was a bar fight, a horrifying accident.

Chance got home and stared at her, bewildered. She sat at the table holding the gun.

"I bought a gun," she said.

"I see that. What for?"

"To shoot. Can we go shooting?"

He put his lunch cooler on the table across from her. "Let's go, it'll be dark soon."

Chance took her to a sandpit on the outskirts of town where townies gathered on Saturday nights to drink cheap beer on the tailgates of their trucks. The target he set up was an empty jug full of sand so she could see when she hit it. He explained the basics to her—breathing, squeezing the trigger and not pulling, pointing the bullet to where she wanted it to go. Chance stood behind her, involved in thoughts he wouldn't reveal if she had asked. The first shot startled her. She almost dropped the gun. It was the sound that bothered her more than the pistol bucking in her hand. All the death she knew had been silent, without the reverie of shouting or anger. The gun was all of that— vicious, barking.

She made him fire the gun while she sat against the hood of her car. When he finished, she motioned him to her with her finger. She smelled the gunpowder on his hand when she took it and pushed her cheek into his palm.

"Why did you ask me about killing the other day?"

"I was drunk, I told you."

"What's the gun for, Audrey?"

"I want to feel protected. I know it's silly, but seeing that guy made me feel unsafe."

"Do you still want to know?"

She paused for a moment then nodded and pushed her cheek against his chest.

"Killing a man makes you feel like you can dig your fingers into the ground and lift the earth over your head. But that only lasts for a moment, and then—" He held his breath.

"Then?"

"Then the blood is sucked from your veins, and the weight of what you've done crushes you."

She slipped her hand beneath his shirt and rubbed her fingers against his body, over the ragged scars on his back. Because of his past, she felt a world apart.

Audrey called out of work the next day. The answering machine at the library took her message, then she drove to Hobbs' camper in Acton. She parked the car where she had the day before and moved slowly through the woods to the back of the camper. The air had become cool, and swirls of rogue snowflakes slipped through the bare branches of the trees. Before Audrey could see the camper, she could smell it. Hobbs fumbled and hacked as he exited the camper and leaned against his picnic table to piss. When he stumbled back inside and made his way to the far end of the camper, she walked quickly across the driveway and stepped inside where the putrid smell of moldy wet towels and urine crawled over her skin. Cigarette burns marred the carpet in a small area near the couch. Empty bottles of booze were scattered everywhere—on counters, cushions, in the open cabinets and on the stove. Hobbs' legs protruded through the doorway of a small room at the end of the camper. She made her way toward him.

He sat in a small chair and looked up at her when she came to the doorway. She had been displaced for so long, no more alive in the world than the books she shelved daily. She'd embraced them because she could leave the tragedy and sorrow within the guts of their pages. If she wanted to experience it, she needed only to grab them by the spine.

She was in control there. And it was a control that had comforted her until she pulled the gun from her pocket. Except for Chance, until that day, she had been a woman of little action, moving through her life the way she did through the library—a steady, somber gait up and down the rows of torment. Until then, she had not forced herself to act on the rage she felt tremble her fingers each morning she awoke. Hobbs stared at her through the glasses that rode crooked on his nose, and she pointed the gun. She heard the sound of his desperate, blinking eyes more than the gunshot. The bullet ripped through his neck and through the pane of glass behind him. Blood chased the bullet only to be cut short by the glass and paneling behind him where it hung for a moment before sliding down the wall. His hacking gurgle was more like the laughter of a small boy in the distance—a sound that required nothing of her emotions for remorse.

Hobbs reached for her, his fingers grabbing clumsily at the air while the fingers of his other hand folded and he dug his knuckles into his cheek. Blood bubbled thick from the wound on his neck and he flung his arm toward her, knocking the glasses from his face. She felt drops of his blood hit her hairline. He arched his back, his calves flexing until the chair he was sitting in toppled over and he fell to the floor. A surge of fecal odor pulsed through the room. She squatted and reached for his glasses on the floor but stopped herself before she touched them. The ringing in her ears hit alternating tones as she moved back to the car. She set her cruise control and pushed her heels into the floorboard in an attempt to stop her knees from shaking.

Chance was washing out his cereal bowl when she entered the house. She had driven the entire way home still gripping the pistol and entered the kitchen with it at her side. He stopped moving his hands and the water splurged from the bowl, showering the counter and the front of his shirt.

"What the hell?"

"I killed him."

Chance tightened his jaw and placed the bowl in the dishrack on the counter. He stopped the water and dried his hands. "You killed who?"

She tried to say his name first. "H-h-him."

Chance gripped the edge of the counter and leaned forward. His shoulders pushed toward his ears. "You shot him?"

She nodded.

"With the gun you just bought?"

She nodded again, adding a quiet groan.

"Did anyone see you?"

She shook her head.

"Did you call out of work?"

Nodding.

He breathed deeply and looked away from her. In a blur of movement, he grabbed the bowl from the rack and threw it against the cabinet doors. It shattered and fell in pieces. His movements then were quick, and his speech was low and controlled—indifferent and lacking the deepness in pitch she was used to.

"Take off your clothes," he told her.

"What?"

He charged at her. "Give me the gun and take your fucking clothes off." He checked the cylinder. "Good, you used the hollow points." He went to a cabinet first and took out a trash bag and threw it at her feet. "Put them in there." He slid the junk drawer open and pulled out a small round file which he slid into the end of the barrel and worked against the metal.

"What are you doing?" She asked, standing in her panties and bra.

"Those too." He pointed at her underwear with the file. He took the bullets from the gun and placed them in a trash bag with her clothes. "If they recover a fragment from the hollow point they can run a ballistics test on, they won't be able to match it to this gun. The file changes the rifling marks. I'm going to vacuum out your car and get rid of this bag. Go get in the shower and stay there. Use the Lava soap I have under the sink and go over yourself at least three times." She held her hands against the small of her stomach and moved slowly through the house.

When she came out of the shower, all but a corner of the mattress hung off the bed. The sheets and comforter were strewn over the bedposts. Her candles had been swept from the top of the dresser. She moved into the living room. Couch cushions were flipped up on the couch. DVDs and CDs were scattered across the floor. In the kitchen, a chair laid on its side. Chance dropped a stack of plates on the floor as she entered.

"Do you know how much I love you, Audrey?"

"What are you doing?"

Chance bit his bottom lip to cease its quivering. He took her by her hand and positioned her in front of the sink. A tear struck the corner of his eye and slid down the edge of his nose.

"Audrey, you fucked up."

"Chance—"

His fist smashed into her cheekbone and she flailed

backwards into the sink. She tried to hold herself steady, but her knees gave out. She crumbled to the floor. Often, she'd wondered how he could have killed someone, what rage he'd embraced to exude that kind of power. She had only ever known his hands to be gentle despite the abuse he put them through. In that instance, she knew just how powerful he was—how crushing and absolute his violence could be if he chose. He stepped closer to her and knelt.

"Audrey, the cops are going to come here and ask you questions. They're going to want to know why you bought a gun, and why the man who killed your brother was killed with the same caliber only days after you bought it. They're going to want to know why you called out of work the day he was killed. You have to have answers to these questions."

She felt her pulse throb through the warmth in her face.

"Listen to me very carefully. With my record, they're not going to doubt your story. You bought the gun because you were scared—because I had gotten violent. I've been violent for months. You called out of work today because I hit you. Now repeat it back to me."

The puffiness in her face was aching. She'd never been hit. The eye was beginning to swell. "I bought the gun because I was afraid. You hit me."

"Good." He reached past her and opened the sink cabinet. "Get the gun."

She pulled the gun out and looked back at him.

"Okay. After you do this, call nine-one-one. Tell them you were in a fight with your boyfriend and he came after you and you shot him."

"What?"

"Listen to me. It'll be okay, I promise. I put .38's in it.

I'll have to go away for a little while, but not long. Just do what I told you to do and stick to the story no matter what. I mean it, no matter what the cops tell you, you stick to the story. I got violent. You got the gun for protection. Got it?"

Audrey nodded. Chance gripped her hand and moved the muzzle of the gun to his chest. He pushed it into the soft part of his flesh just inside his shoulder below his collarbone. She felt the tension in his hand keeping her grip on the gun.

"This is important. If the cops ask you about anything else besides what we talked about, you lawyer up.

She was crying, and Chance kissed her cheek.

"This will bring us closer."

He pushed her index finger against the trigger with his thumb.

"Closer"—Thin Ice: Crime Fiction by New England Writers

Across the alley, Rick and Alice began to fight. Their son Benny scrambled through the apartment for his mittens and coat and hat and let himself out of the apartment. "Motherfucker" was the only word Jeremy could make out through the telephoto lens on his camera. He snapped away, catching various poses of their lips as they projected the invective toward each other. It wouldn't take long for Rick to drop her with a right hook. Jeremy had seen that half a dozen times already.

For two weeks he'd been watching them, and it wouldn't have been different than any other drug investigation except the captain kept him on surveillance no matter how much evidence he collected against Rick Stallings. Buyers went to Rick, and Jeremy took their pictures. They were an indiscriminate mix of people whose likeness was their desire. Base-heads arrived with their infected gums and their money crumpled and dirty, frat-boys with cashmere-cotton blend sweaters and the crisp bills they'd received from the ATM, blue-collar guys on payday so they could stay up and get the most out of their drinking time, hookers in need of making the most out of their working hours, and meticulous housewives who would have run out of energy by noon without it. They all knocked on the door with their reasons and needs. They all made their contributions to that social dynamic. They all gave Jeremy a reason other than his divorce to be stuck in that crummy, third-floor apartment.

The apartment was on the back end of the building and overlooked a dead-end alley that businesses had used for deliveries. There were no businesses at that end of town anymore. Even the bustle of rats had diminished to a few struggling survivors. The apartments were all the same—shitty carpet stained with piss, vomit and blood, and the walls dropped strips of paint from corroding sheetrock. There was the constant sound of running water and crying and screaming. Jeremy snapped a few more shots of Rick and Alice then put the camera down.

A bottle of whiskey sat within arm's reach, unopened. He'd quit drinking to save his marriage, but Mally left anyway, without a goodbye or a note. Nothing except her small footprints leading up to the street being filled with falling snow by the time he'd gotten home. He'd walked through the empty house with the one-month sobriety chip he'd just received and a wallet-size card that had the serenity prayer on one side and a poem about footprints on the other. The times when you had seen only one set of footprints in the sand was when I carried you. Jeremy thought about the card, whispered "bullshit" and lifted the camera. Footprints began where angels dropped you, if you landed on your feet, the weight of you unwanted, your prayers a burden on the ear of God.

Rick and Alice circled around the small wooden table.

Rick had pulled his shirt open. Jeremy put the camera to his eye. The lens brought the eagle tattoo on Rick's chest into focus—poorly done and faded on his left pec. Alice was wearing a white T-shirt and light blue panties. Her thighs flexed as she moved toward Rick on the balls of her feet. She had bony shoulders and thin arms—her fingers delicate and long. She looked good, Jeremy thought—as sleek and elegant as the stainless-steel paring knife she was holding. Jeremy wished she'd sink it in Rick's neck or get lucky and poke him between the ribs. Alice threw the knife at Rick, which he swatted away. She went to the refrigerator and pulled the revolver from the top of it. Rick moved slowly with his arms out.

Jeremy put the camera down again. He didn't want any evidence against Alice if she decided to dump a round or two into Rick's chest. They stood for a moment until Alice began to cry and Rick pulled the gun from her hand and the two hugged. Jeremy put on some jeans and sat in the corner of the apartment on a milk crate. He put on his boots and secured them with duct tape after the laces broke. The tread had been worn flat, and the leather was soft, like a moccasin. Jeremy tore the few pages of notes from the pad on the counter, folded them around the camera's memory card and stuffed them into his back pocket. The last gulp of coffee was cold and he spit it into the sink. He put on a long john shirt, a black hooded sweatshirt, a thigh-length black leather jacket, a black beanie and gloves.

Metal chattered against metal as Jeremy made his way down the ladder of the fire escape to the alley below. His exhaled breaths chugged through the rungs as he descended. Benny, Alice's kid, was circling on his bicycle until his back tire caught a patch of ice and the bike kicked out from under him. The boy toppled to the pavement at Jeremy's feet and quickly recovered.

"Sorry, mister," the boy said and jerked his bike upright by the handlebars.

Jeremy rubbed the end of his nose with two of his fingers, adjusting it to the cold. He studied the kid's face, wondering how old he would be before black eyes and split lips would start appearing. Jeremy pulled his jacket tighter and made his way to the end of the alley. The gray and brown brick multiple-story buildings stood around him. Clouds hovered low in the sky, rippled like corrugated roofs. Snow, dirty with car exhaust and sand, clung to the base of the sidewalks and buildings. The streets were narrow, even more so with the mounds of snow pushed to the side by plow trucks and left there so the city could impose parking bans and spend the night towing.

O'Connor's, the corner store, was two blocks down on the right. He stopped there every morning for a cup of coffee on his way to the park. O'Connor scratched his neck and sighed more than anyone really had to when Jeremy pulled change from his pocket, coin by coin, to pay for the coffee. O'Connor got his knees broken by a scar-faced Irishman after a bad bet on the '85 Super Bowl. He hobbled around with a cane on the rare occasions he wasn't nested behind the counter.

"Coffee'd be cheaper if you made it at home," O'Connor said to Jeremy.

"Then I'd have no place to get rid of all this extra change."

"You could take it up the hill and give it to the panhandlers."

"They don't sell coffee." Jeremy smiled.

O'Connor shook his head and swept the change from the counter into his palm.

Jeremy waited for the captain behind the high school at Grant Field. The remaining faculty made their way to the staff parking lot. Some of them lit cigarettes as they fled school property. Wind rolled a wave of glistening white over the snow-covered field. Jeremy dumped the rest of his coffee when the captain arrived. The captain remained wrapped in his wool peacoat, a tan scarf wrapped tightly around his neck, and his hands and fingers gloved in calfskin despite the heat in the vehicle. His hair was gray, even the well-manicured goatee. His eyes were bright and focused because he slept at night.

"The snaps were good yesterday," The captain said after Jeremy closed the passenger-side door.

"The part where Rick Stallings smacked his kid around?"

"We're not here for that, Jeremy."

"This doesn't feel right. I've taken more pictures than an Asian tourist. How long am I going to be on this?"

"Stallings has slipped through our fingers twice. I'm not taking another chance of him being acquitted."

"You didn't have this kind of evidence last time."

"If I remember right, the last time you made a bust, a bartender testified that you were drunk when you made the arrest."

Jeremy pulled his hat lower over his ears. "I've been sober three months."

"Let's keep it that way. You been to any meetings?"

"What, and miss an eight-round amateur bout with Stallings and his wife?"

"Don't get fucking smart with me. You're lucky you're

still a cop."

Jeremy fished the memory card from his pocket and placed it on the seat between him and the captain. "I'd better get back."

The captain spoke when Jeremy pulled on the door handle. "Hang on, kid. I didn't mean to be so hard on you. Just keep doing what you're doing. This will all be over soon."

Jeremy smirked. "You mean, eventually."

He climbed from the captain's car and followed his footprints from the day before across the field, a single unwavering set through the snow. He stopped to look back only when he'd reached the other side before he scrambled up the banking. The captain's car was long gone.

Jeremy walked by his childhood home. New families had moved in, grown and left. He walked down to the sandpit, where his father had driven the car that night—where he'd escaped from the car over the bits of broken glass from the window he'd shattered with his hands—where his father's life ended in the front seat of the car with pills and carbon monoxide while his mother's body lay in the trunk.

Benny sat in his room on a plastic-lined mattress, coloring the outside edges of his coloring book around the figures that had been colored before Jeremy got there to watch Rick. The crayons were worn down, and Benny made his choice of color by the smell of them—held them to his nose and sniffed, then tossed the unwanted back into the small plastic baggie. Benny turned through the pages of his coloring book—each page colored to the edges. He climbed off the bed and pushed his dresser away from the wall and started a mural. He'd chosen a forest green crayon and drew a tree—the shape of a cookie-cutter Christmas tree. After he finished off the green crayon, he moved to a red one and began to color circles at the tips of the pointed branches.

Rick moved through the apartment, and Benny pushed the dresser back and leapt to his bed. The blood vessels swelled on Rick's neck until they were throbbing and more of them swelled and branched out on his forehead as if something crawled beneath his skin and his expression was pain and not anger. Benny pushed himself against the headboard and flinched when Rick snatched the coloring book and rolled it up. But that was all that Benny did in the way of defending himself. When Rick went to thwacking Benny with the book, Benny rolled to his stomach and relaxed, whimpering into his bag of crayons and wetting the peeled paper with tears. Rick tossed the coloring book next to Benny where it unraveled like the wings of a spine-injured bird. Benny sat up after a moment and dug through the crayons. He took what was left of the black one and went back to the mural behind the dresser. He slashed through the tree with angry strokes until the crayon was gone.

Alice tugged on Benny's arm the next morning on their way down to the bus stop. Jeremy hung back a block and watched the boy slap his lunch box off the back of his leg. His backpack was puffed out with air and looked far too large for the small boy. In his other hand, Benny carried the plastic baggie full of used, paper-pulled crayons.

* * *

On surveillance, the worst acts are never the reason for watching. Abuse, rape, even murder were sometimes ancillary to the purpose. The victims were significant only when they served their purpose, when they provided what was needed. Sometimes, rapists and abusers and murderers were sent to prison. There, they paid their debt to society while the victims remained vulnerable and scavenging for justice or hope or faith. And God judged the wicked, giving value to their life while the victims served only a purpose for that judgment.

That evening, Benny sat on his bed holding the revolver in his palms. He aimed it ahead of him with both hands wrapped around the grip, his elbows out and his head sunk between his shoulders to look down the sight. Benny straightened up and looked down at the revolver again. He swung the gun around him, taking aim at different points of the room. Benny grew more confident with the weight of the gun and stood on the bed. He attempted to spin it on his finger. Jeremy could feel the muscle fibers between his ribs tighten. The gun fell to the mattress. Jeremy put the camera down. Benny retrieved the gun and made another attempt.

The gunshot popped, muffled by the walls and the window of Benny's room. His small body pushed against the tension of the glass for a quick moment before it quit on him and let him fall. The fabric of his clothing bloated with the air forcing between the threads. His eyes were closed, and the shocked expression remained on Benny's face as he moved through the air, his body limp as it drifted down. Glass sang against the ground like the song of wind chimes from a gentle breeze. A muted thump. One quick, hideous sigh rose through the alley when the boy hit, sending a cloud of snow dust curling and billowing around his body, rising half the distance that he had fallen.

Alice burst into Benny's room. She braced herself against the wooden frame of the broken window. The remaining shards of glass cut into her flesh as she screamed down the alley for her son—reaching out as if she were lunging for his hand to save him. Her reach caught only the brisk wind against the cuts on her palms.

Only the people moving by on the sidewalks stopped to peer into the alley. In the windows of other apartments, where there was movement and where Jeremy was positive that they'd heard, he waited to see the curtains flutter, but nothing.

Jeremy slipped down to the floor, gazing at the chaotic scars on his hands, like worms crawling over the pavement after rain. He leaned against the cabinet of the sink long after the ambulance had come and spurt its spinning lights through his window, after the various voices of the crowd had twined themselves into an inconsiderate whine, after the beeps and static crackles of communication devices had slipped into the night to report other tragedies.

"This shouldn't have happened," Jeremy said. He stared through the windshield of the captain's car—his lips parted slightly, a dark, empty look in his eyes.

The captain turned the heater dial down. The air blowing in the car diminished.

"Jeremy, this was a horrible tragedy. Nobody could have seen this coming."

"If we'd busted Stallings a week ago, we wouldn't have had to see it coming."

"No. We're not superheroes. We can't prevent the death of every innocent person out there. Rick's going to meet with his suppliers. Focus on that, Jeremy. You make this case and your previous debacle will be ancient history. I promise this will be over soon."

Jeremy looked down to the scars on his hands. "Like everything else," he said.

"Should I be concerned about you?"

"In what way?"

"I'm concerned about how this affects you. I can't risk blowing this operation."

"You'll get Rick Stallings, Captain. Don't lose any sleep."

Rick and Alice didn't fight for three days. People arrived with their needs, to receive and scurry away to feed their own tragedies, to meet the conformity of their own agendas. They passed their money into Rick's hands and he rewarded them with the treasures they so desperately sought. Jeremy clenched the still unopened bottle of whiskey he'd kept on the counter next to his notes and his camera and the binoculars waiting for whatever was going to happen.

On the day of the funeral, Rick moved through the apartment, gathering money from his various hiding places. He loaded money into a duffel bag from the crisper drawer in the refrigerator, the top shelf of the cupboard and from beneath a loose floorboard in his closet. Alice came from the shower wrapped in a towel and sat next to the black dress she had laid across her bed. Her hair was wet, matted together and heavy on her shoulders. She rested the back of her bandaged hands on her thighs and stared blankly through the doorway of her bedroom. Alice's body trembled while she dressed.

The funeral was held in a large cathedral church—the parking lot as grand in size but nearly empty. Jeremy waited for the stragglers smoking near the entrance to go inside before following them. The pews sprawled beneath the large space of the church. Benny's casket was displayed beyond the pews, small enough to require only four pallbearers, and in the grand space of the church it seemed ridiculed because of its tininess.

He fought his urge to weep until he made it home and opened the bottle. Then, after he'd lifted it and smelled the relief it had promised in whispers since he'd stopped drinking, the urge was gone. Jeremy licked his dry lips and put the bottle down. He posted himself over the sink and waited, looking through the alley at Alice and her bandaged palms pressing against her eyes.

Rick opened the door for his suppliers and, despite their black apparel and hats pulled low over their foreheads, Jeremy could tell they were cops—Evans and Kittredge. Jeremy sighed, and the duties the captain had given him made more sense. He'd fucked up his last bust, and the captain had given him a chance to make sure this bust was righteous. Jeremy punched the button of the camera until his knuckle cramped and he switched to using his middle finger. When he filled the memory card, he quickly replaced it and snapped away again.

Six pictures into the new card, when Rick Stallings cut a small hole in the bag of blow to test the quality, Kittredge left the apartment. What the hell? Jeremy thought. Before an answer came to him, Evans slipped a small, silenced .380 from inside his jacket and put the barrel in Rick's face. Evans shot twice and went into the hallway. Jeremy paused, almost dropped the camera but lifted it and kept snapping. Evans moved into the bedroom where Alice sat on the bed and shot her twice before she could see anything more than a flash in her peripheral vision.

Jeremy chambered a round into his Glock as he pounded down the fire escape. When his boots hit the pavement, a shadow spun from beneath the metal stairs. Another hit struck Jeremy's gut, then his arm. Jeremy dropped his gun and gasped for air as he went to the ground. Kittredge tossed the pipe he'd swung into a dumpster and scooped up the pistol Jeremy was reaching for. The hollow thumps of his heart droned through his chest.

Evans came into the alley before Jeremy could catch his breath. The two of them dragged him to a dumpster and pushed him against the brick. Their breaths twisted together and rose into the night as they stood above him. The streetlight at the end of the alley shined over their backs and shoulders and shadowed their faces. When they started on him, each punch brought a still-frame memory of the things he'd seen—the heated metal coat hangers charring lines into the flesh of an infant's face, the father opening the door to his twelve-year-old daughter's room in trade for a fifteen-minute fix, the bubbles subsiding in a tub of water where a mother held her child because it wouldn't stop crying. They couldn't hit him enough for his memories to run out. He'd been a spectator, a participant in the creation of victims. Jeremy savored the pain in his bones from where they'd hit him. It had been a long time since he'd been hit like that—a long time since he had curled into a ball and prayed for God to stop the hitting, but there was no begging this time, and Jeremy took what they had to give him until everything went numb and dark.

When Jeremy came to, he could tell he'd been in the car

for a while. Kittredge was asleep against the window in the seat in front of him. Evans stared over the wheel like he was fitting the car between a tight space. The person next to him cracked the seal on a liquor bottle. Jeremy knew that sound—relief. He straightened himself the best he could against the ache in his temples and looked over at the captain.

"Take a drink, Jeremy," he said, holding out a pint of bottom-shelf bourbon.

A flash of heat burned in Jeremy's gut. He remembered the stoic look of his father the night he drove them to the sandpit. The captain, though, his stoic look shared a seat with comfort, and Jeremy had finally made sense of it all.

"Good payday, Captain?" Jeremy asked.

"Just drink the fucking booze, kid."

Jeremy took the bottle. "Where are we?"

"The County," Evans said.

"Interesting."

Evans leaned back in his seat. "Not as interesting as the murders you committed."

"I didn't kill anyone."

The captain sparked a match and lit a cigarette. "You killed yourself a long time ago, kid."

Jeremy turned his head from the captain and tipped the bottle. When he finished his drink, he sucked the taste from his teeth. "My fingerprints are all over the surveillance equipment. Smart move, Captain. This wasn't even a sanctioned investigation, was it?"

The captain blew smoke over Evans' shoulder.

"Why me?" Jeremy asked.

"Convenience, Jeremy. Plausibility. Simplicity. Choose whatever reason you want."

Eventually, the car slowed and stopped at a gated road. Kittredge got out and opened the gate. When Evans pulled past, Kittredge closed it. He crossed behind the car and got in, squeezing his hands together for warmth.

Farther down the road they stopped, and Kittredge pulled Jeremy from the back seat. The moon lit the hard, packed snow on the road. The white gleamed in the light until it faded into darkness ahead where the road curved out of sight or simply ended. The other men climbed from the car, Evans eager to put Jeremy down. The captain fanned his jacket open and worked the buttons closed. Evans pulled his throwaway piece from his ankle holster— a dingy snub nose revolver like the one Benny had become a victim to, nothing special or significant, only something to serve its purpose.

"Any last words?" Evans asked and waited for Jeremy to respond. When he didn't, he motioned Jeremy forward with a tilt of his head.

Firs shaded the ground from the light of the moon on each side of the road. Jeremy stepped beneath the darkness of the tree branches, hearing his footsteps pack the snow. Ahead of him, the darkness slashed through the trees— nothing, peace. With his first couple of steps he thought of the sheet of plywood that covered Benny's window, the bull's eye his death had left on the ground. He continued to walk. With each step, he felt increasingly light. When spring came, his footprints would melt away. There would be no indication that he had walked. It would be as if he had fallen there in the spot where the bullets roared through the cold air and brought him down.

"The Fallen"—Dead Calm: Crime Fiction by New England Writers

Marie needs to watch something die. She's on the bed, naked, when I come into the room. The scars on her wrists are dark even in the dim light. I've watched her do this before, take sharp pencils and pull the erasers out with her teeth, then bite the metal band into a point to cut herself. She'd spin in circles around the room, letting her blood cast in small drops on lamp shades and torn pages of the Gideon's scattered on the floor. She looks up at me and bites her lip until it splits. I close the door and nod. Her eyes water and she smears the blood with the bottom of her tongue. She sits up on the bed and trails a stethoscope over the sheets.

"I want to know," she says.

Marie once told me not to fall in love, that we learn to hate the ones we love because it helps us feel less when we hurt them.

I close my eyes and I can see her in a wedding dress, the neck of a whiskey bottle clenched in her hand, while she walks the double yellow lines on a sharp curve, barefoot, light snow falling through an icy wind, her skin blued with the pain she's gained the ability to ignore. A Mac truck swings around the curve, the tires of one side lifting slightly off the ground with its speed.

One day, you're going to be a man, Ross promised. It was the only thing he'd said to me when we left the fights. He'd said that and shook his head while I looked at myself in the mirror of his '82 Dodge pickup, my face the young, unscarred patina of a future monster. The truck wobbled and squeaked, and it was just as run down as Ross. Ross wasn't much of a fighter, and whatever level of toughness he wanted to exude was presented vicariously through his dogs. I was only ten years old at the time, old enough to know that Ross wasn't my real father. When he pulled into the driveway, I slid from the truck, hoping Scrap was going to be okay.

Scrap cowered in the cage that Ross kept in the rotten plywood bed of the Dodge. He yanked Scrap by the leash out of his cage and Scrap hit the ground with a thump between us. Ross fed the hand loop of the leash through the space between the bumper. He tied the leash off and walked to the side of the pickup, where he reached into his cooler for a beer. My mother came from the house, a small, white two-bedroom ranch with slanted floors and crooked windows that made more noise than Ross' truck.

"How'd it go?" she asked.

Ross looked my mother up and down. I looked, too, at the bruises on her arms from his grip, the puffy cheekbone on the right side of her face, her swollen bottom lip and the faint purple hue on her chin.

"Scrap lost," Ross answered. He took a swig of beer

and stared down at the dog and then me with the same glare of resentment. Scrap, indifferent to his torn ear, the gash in his shoulder and the flap of hide that hung from his neck, licked the back of my hand.

"That's a shame."

Ross tipped his beer up and finished it. "Shame, alright. You go on in, now. I'm gon' teach your boy about being a man."

The smile left my mother's face and she sulked back into the house. When the door closed behind her, Ross pushed himself from the truck with his elbows, an unopened beer in one hand and a two-foot length of pipe in the other.

I met Marie at the same place I met everyone else in every other town I moved through. I don't forget how I meet these people, and when I move on, it's always the same. Same people, same story, same scarred and hopeless cannibals feeding off the same things that made them victims.

"We're going back to my place," she told me on her way out. It was the first thing she'd said to me. Kevin and Max, brothers who had an interest in similar things from painkillers to pre-pubescent girls, followed Marie. They both looked like they'd been used for punching bags and their thin skin was just a narrow sack for their broken bones.

We all smoked cigarettes in Marie's room in a highway hotel just off of Route 11, a dingy, damp carpet and sticky sheets kind of place, much like the kind of places my mother and I lived in when we fled Alabama, when it was her turn to teach me how to be a man. I sat close to the window in Marie's room but kept myself from looking past the curtain. I did it once and Kevin's scowl made me want to tie him in a knot.

Marie asked me where I was from, what I did to become an offender, and they chewed on my lies like they were the first few jaw strokes of flavored gum. I'm not an offender, not in the way that Max and Kevin and Marie are offenders. I don't have to register. I'm not in any database, and nobody knows my real name is Michael. Marie let Kevin and Max turn themselves inside out on Oxy and meth, handing each other a blood-tipped rolled dollar bill through the smoke. Max ground at the six teeth he had left, which were hued with the bluish tint of rot waiting to break through old fillings.

"How do you get by?" Marie finally asked.

"However I can," I answered. Kevin and Max's breathing came through the room like soft whispers. I pressed out a cigarette in a small glass ashtray on the battered table by the window.

"Panhandle?"

"Sometimes," I nodded. I watched their eyes. "I usually go a little dirtier than that."

Kevin and Max stopped their breathing to look at Marie. She let a half smile come to her mouth, a twitch at the corner of her eyes, and she pulled a long hard drag off her cigarette, enough to force the cherry to peel half of it back. I said nothing else, and a little while later, Marie told Kevin and Max to leave.

I didn't know what it was to be a man until I'd been hate-fucked by a woman, until I felt responsible for her damage solely because of my sex.

* * *

Scrap didn't cry for help. Ross took turns pushing me to the side and swinging that pipe down on him. Each time Ross pushed me, Scrap lunged, snapped his jaw in the air just before he was jerked back by his own leash. Finally, Scrap collapsed, growling into the dirt. Ross tossed the pipe into the back of the Dodge where it clanged against the tire chains. He climbed into the cab. The engine started, and I tried to reach for the bumper as he pulled off through the field to the edge of the wood line. Scrap lurched away and scrambled in an attempt to get to his feet. I ran behind the truck, screaming for Ross to stop, crying, and my eyes so blurred I had to follow Scrap's yelps and the gunning of the engine, the rich, oil-burning stench of the exhaust.

When the truck stopped, I fell to the ground where Scrap whimpered, and his big, brown eyes looked over at me as I panted. Scrap pushed himself closer to me, yelping from the pressure on his broken front legs, lashing his tongue out toward my face, flicking dust and dirt into my eyes. Ross pulled something from his glove box and came out to the back of the truck. Scrap snarled, bearing his last bits of energy through a dry mouth and broken teeth. Ross picked me up by the collar of my T-shirt, then gripped my chin with a fat, dry hand. My tears soaked the calluses on his fingers, and he wiped his hand against his pant legs and pulled the revolver from his back pocket.

For six weeks, I stayed with Marie, breathing in the smell of sweat and smoke and the burning plastic that wafted in from another room. Each night ended like the first, after she told the boys to leave. She'd sit on her bed, pulling her hair into pigtails. Other times, she'd start to color on the walls with crayons she'd taken a handful of from the basket at Friendly's and tell me to put her over my knee. Then there were the playgrounds at night and the back seats of cars when we parked near toy stores.

We pulled off three jobs during that time. Kevin and Max's grandmother's house yielded nothing more than worthless collectibles that the two swore were priceless. The high school office proved to be more lucrative than I expected, but only giving the four of us a little over $200 that Kevin and Max spent on crank and Q-tips and Vaseline.

During the third job, Marie pulled me out into the garage of the house we were ransacking while Kevin and Max looted the place. Her cotton Care Bears panties shredded like a worn, gas-soaked shop rag and her round white ass gleamed under the fluorescent light above. I had her pinned down over oily tools strewn over the small workbench—the boards layered with the thick gunk of car fluids and grease. Inside her, I felt the weak muscles flex, and the even weaker ones in her neck push against the grip I had on the back of her skull. She whimpered, and the hair over her face kept me from knowing if she was smiling or gritting her teeth in pain. When I finished, she righted herself slowly. Her knees gave slightly with the adjustment of different pressure—the indent of a metric wrench on the side of her face like a burn scar. Her legs shook, and she slid her hands over her thighs in an attempt to push some calm into her stance. I pulled my pants back up and took a long look at her eyes, waiting for the light above her to show some sign of life.

"Have you ever killed?" she asked.

* * *

We went to the carnival that night. She walked feverishly through the people in the crowd. I followed, a few feet behind her, blending into the purposeless gait of fair attendees who binged on fried dough and onion blooms. Marie walked in circles around the entire carnival, around the Ferris wheel and carousel, the animal pens and the performance stages, through the rows and rows of rigged games. We walked over the lines of shadows, watched the people around us laugh and grunt and push.

She finally stopped beside a food stand and stared at the lightless space on the other side of the fairground fencing where the cars were parked. She stared and I watched her thoughts come through on her face in twitches and tension until she'd squinted tears from her eyes and that squint expanded into the ugly mask of her agenda. I let her cry, gave her the space to absorb her thoughts.

"I have a job for us," she said.

"What?

"He's a doctor, was a doctor, but he's holding, and he'll have paper."

A man knows when it's— Ross' voice trailed off and I took the gun he'd held out for me and shot the dog between the eyes before he could finish. Scrap fell still at my feet. Ross looked down at me and nodded, his voice coming back into the fold. *You're a man, now.*

I pushed the barrel into his stomach and pulled the trigger again.

He crawled away from me after he'd collapsed, cussing

me, holding both of his hands against his stomach just to the left of his navel. I stepped over the dog and moved toward Ross, lifting the gun and letting the barrel hover and point at his top lip.

I stared at him, watched him fade, felt nothing, except a purpose.

I went to the doctor's with a brick, shattered the sliding glass door in the back and pulled the crowbar from my belt. Kevin and Max trailed behind me. The former doctor came from the living room—tall, lanky, in a white button-down. His pleated khakis were wrinkled at the knees. His face bore the look of shock and curiosity. As I backed the doctor into the living room with the point of my crowbar, I caught the short movement of the closet door closing halfway—a little girl slinking back behind the jackets. The doctor watched her, a brief flex of annoyance coming to his face.

I pulled the gun from my waistband, a shiny, forty-caliber Berretta, more intimidating than the .32 in my jacket pocket. Max and Kevin shifted with excitement.

Soft, delicate fabric and the animal print that littered the doctor's home indicated the flare of a woman's decorating touch, but the pizza boxes and open milk container on the counter, the slacks and shirts tossed over the backs of dining room chairs, the corners of *Barely Legal* magazines poking from beneath the couch and the small pile of Flunitrazepam and Viagra told me that the woman wasn't around anymore.

The boys split up and went through the house, looking for the stash that Marie said was there. They tossed artwork and pictures off the walls, dumped glass and dishes and food from cabinets. They sliced mattresses and pillows. They tossed them out into the hallway and the stairwell. They tore apart stuffed animals. The little girl panted sobs into her forearm.

Max and Kevin abandoned their search and returned to the living room, shaking their heads. I could smell Max's breath from behind me, a putrid stench like he'd eaten something dead and let it rot more in the heat of his guts.

"Where's the stash?" Kevin tapped the crowbar against his gloved palm.

"I, I, I don't know what you're talking about. Stash?"

I pushed the safety off on the Beretta and pointed it at the doctor's face. "Two seconds."

"Where's the fucking Oxy, Doc?" Max asked, sniffing hard and rubbing his gloved palm in a circular motion over his nose, his breathing raspy through the cloth of his ski mask.

The doctor shook his head and kept his eyes focused on the closet. In the mirror behind him, I saw the little girl's fingers grip around the sleeves of a jacket.

"I don't know what you're talking about."

Max asked, "Where's the girl?"

Marie had said too much.

The doctor's head tilted, his chin moved up and he pushed his lower lip toward his teeth. And it was then that I noticed the resemblance, why Marie didn't come. Time lurched to a halt at my feet, derailed—steel buckled and snapped, and I saw the cars of past days come off the tracks and tumble to the side in gnarled wreckage.

I pulled the trigger. The shots ripped through the house like the paper bags Kevin popped after he huffed keyboard cleaner or spray paint.

On the floor, the doctor lay sprawled out with his neck twisted against the weight of his head and the awkward fall through the coffee table.

Max tapped my shoulder with a crowbar. "You're the man," he said. "Where's the girl, though?" he pleaded. "I want to see the girl. Where is that little bitch?"

"Go wait in the bathroom. I'll find her," I told them. I pulled a small plastic pouch from my back pocket. Max snatched it and Kevin followed him up the stairs.

When they disappeared around the corner at the top of the stairs, I moved.

The girl bit into the knuckle of my forefinger when I handed her the phone. There was snapping and I wondered if it was the sound of plastic hangers from the coats that fell while she struggled or my finger. She looked over the black shroud that hid my face. She focused in on my eyes, and I on hers. The redness in her sclera spiraled down to a thin ring of blue and the thick black pulsing of her pupil. I pulled my finger from her teeth and closed the closet door.

The boys were leaning over the edge of the sink as I stepped into the doorway of the bathroom. Kevin pulled away from his line and Max dipped for his. Kevin smiled, and it was the last expression he offered. When I left the bathroom, I closed the door and sirens in the distance clashed with the gunshots ringing in my ears.

I buried Scrap in the loose dirt at the edge of Ross' land, where the Kudzu crawled over the stone wall like an infiltrating purge of botanical assault. I spit at Ross' feet while I dug, glaring at his pudgy face, the open mouth. I curled

Scrap into his usual sleeping position against the rocks I'd placed at the base of his grave. I covered him with stones before I filled the hole with dirt and packed it down. I took one more look at Ross, spit against his cheek and watched it slide over the corner of his mouth before I walked through the dying grass back to the house.

Marie whimpers against the sheets. She turns her head to face the mirror so she can watch. I tighten my grip on the rubber tube of the stethoscope she wrapped around her neck, pulling it tighter, and the darkness in her eyes starts to fade. It will all fade now—the paths of our purpose, the line that cuts the shape of our form into man or woman, that separates damage and redemption. Her voice echoes and flitters through the room softer and softer.

DRINK TILL YOU'RE GONE

You haven't said a word in three hours. You sit on the edge of the river, the Mousam, watching the murky ripples on the shoreline, and you think about her. The scene comes back over and over in your head: door open; scattered shreds of newspaper strewn across the carpet; the solemn grin of the bar in the empty closet; the cool, hollow feeling of a barren house.

She'd planned it, had it down to the last few ashes that drifted into the air when you nudged the ashtray on the carpet just inside the door.

For a moment, you see her waiting there at the door, sitting against the frame and smoking—the way she used to do when she still loved you. You bought her that ashtray for a dime at a yard sale on your first date. She got tired of waiting.

You imagine a task force of two-man teams sweeping through the house to move the couch, dresser, washing machine, dryer, kitchen table, boxes. Their echoes grew louder as the house emptied. Quick footsteps shook the panes of glass in the windows as they made a final sweep for the curtains, silverware and the contents of the medicine cabinet. Men who breathed quietly, without effort, erased her from the apartment. It was a shithole anyway. Even more now that the sunlight spilled in on the vacant places you fought or fucked. You stepped back outside, watched the neighbors duck back into their houses. Then you came here, to the edge of the river, to the bench where you proposed, trying to figure out what you're going to do in what little time you have left.

You should go get a drink. Put on a show for the men following you. She's not coming back. You take a moment to think about where your life shifted, where you adopted the delusion that things would go your way. You try to find a starting point—first day of school, a childhood birthday, the moment you decided to snitch. You'll start when you get to the bar, when you get a drink, like you always do.

Gutter. You can smell the bar behind you, hear the click of heels on the sidewalk as people pass. Someone drops a few of quarters on the cement next to you. Your lips are swollen, and you remember how you got there. You might have made it on your own, but someone helped you. They helped you because you helped yourself to the beer in front of him when the bartender cut you off. You crumbled in the corner where you looked at the floor wondering where it came from. You saw your blood on his fist, felt it pool below your tongue. Then you crawled outside, over the sticky barroom floor, the damp peanut shells and small, gelling pools of dip spit.

You do your best to scratch the dried blood from your

lips. A shadow stretches over your legs and you turn your head.

"Got some identification?" the cop asks.

You reach for your wallet, squint against the glare, hand it up to him.

The pounding in your head—you can feel it, hear its approach like the footsteps of Mormons or Jehovah's, the only people who have made an effort to talk to you in the last two months.

He says your name, as if you've forgotten. In the gutter, the stink of vomit on your breath, the fuzzy coating on your teeth—the sound of your own name is like a gunshot.

The cop tells you to move on. You make the necessary effort to get to your feet and start walking. The headache starts creeping over your eyeballs. Horns blare, people talk loudly into their phones as you pass. The headache is almost too much, and you barely make it home without throwing yourself in front of a bus or the car that's been following you.

Back at your house, you sit there in the empty space. You go to the window and lift your hand out of habit to move a curtain that is no longer there. You see the car parked across the street. You sit in the corner of the room at the base of the stairwell and watch the sunlight coming through the window onto the carpet and over that ten-cent ashtray fade and the dim gets darker.

Men and women in nylon jackets mill around your body and the red sinking into the carpet, a burgundy stain for the sun to shed some light on. They speak quietly, but their voices echo in the emptiness of the house. They stuff your body into a black bag and zip it up. They lift you to a gurney and push you from the house like furniture for the curb.

You get up and go to the window and move the shade. The room is modest, and you'll be there for a while. It's bright, a yellow—almost gold—bright, and the pain in your head is gone. You glance out the window like you did the day you died. You miss your wife. You wished you had told her how pretty she was while you could. You turn to face the U.S. Marshal pouring himself a cup of coffee. He grins at you and steps over to the table to lift an envelope. He puts the mug down and takes out the documents.

He holds out the picture ID paper-clipped to other papers you're not ready to look at. Your new name—a sound you'll try to memorize when you can look in the mirror again. "Life is short," he tells you. "Make the most of this one."

SPRAWL

Halitosis. Jude smelled it the moment Linda asked to speak with him when he entered the VFW. The stench of it rolled off her tongue behind plaque-drenched teeth and stuck to the inside of his nostrils like wet ash. Jude thumbed his nose as she spoke.

"You haven't been happy here for a long time," she said. "And we've had some issues with cleanliness."

By cleanliness, she meant the Crock-Pots full of chili that he always forgot to put away before closing up the VFW bar. He made no effort to disagree or even realize the opportunity to plea for his job. The only effort he made was to hold his breath and wish he could sink deeper in the clothes that hadn't been too large for him a month before. Linda sat on the desk next to the computer monitor and mimicked its squatty, dust-covered stance. When she asked for his key, the situation was evident, and he pulled his keys from his pocket and stripped the brass door key from the key ring. Linda, breathing a bit heavier, extended her hand, and Jude dropped his key into the thick padding of her palm. He felt his pulse strumming on the insides of

99

his ears begging him to breathe. He slid his hand along the tight, bony corner of his jaw and through his hair.

"I have your money," Linda said and reached over her shoulder to pull an envelope from the shelf above the computer. Jude took the opportunity to exhale and breathe in, dizzied for a moment by the surge of relief shooting through his brain. He took his money. Three hundred dollars for the hours he'd worked over the past two weeks, the hours he'd spent away from Molly's disdain, from her lectures about his inability to provide the life she deserved—for her and the baby.

When they weren't bitching about the *liberal faggots* who'd elected their *non-American* president, the men who'd been to Korea, Vietnam or Kuwait would repeat the same story they'd told him over and over about the deer they'd killed or the women they'd fucked in the ass. Jude pretended, once or twice, to be interested, but ass fucking and shooting an animal killed by more drivers every year than hunters wasn't worth the dollar tip they'd leave him after five hours of drinking. The only truly disheartening thing about losing his job was how Molly would react. Jude could barely afford the small rent payment on their trailer, and he had promised they'd move on once they had enough money.

Jude had worked a better job in Ohio, but he'd gotten Molly pregnant while she was still with her husband and they'd fled in a mix of fear and lust and excitement that vanished as soon as Molly walked into the trailer and saw where she'd be living. His '89 Chevy Corsica had made it as far as Winton, New Hampshire, after what money he'd had in his pocket ran out. Molly hated Winton, and Jude couldn't blame her, but no one knew where that place was. If anyone drifted through, they'd try their best to forget and hurry back to their cozy little towns where the dogs shit on the sidewalks or the front lawns instead of in the middle of the street.

Outside, the sun was setting, and he listened to the whine of snowmobile engines coming up the valley where the cold rushed toward him. Jude walked home, turning his face from the lunging bite of the wind whenever it came close to his cheek.

Molly was gone when he arrived, which confused him. They didn't know anyone and hadn't had the chance to meet people. The closest neighbors were three miles away, across the valley on the other ridge.

Jude stepped into the kitchen, slipped on a piece of waxy wrapper and caught himself against the counter. He picked it up and dropped it into the trash bin where the purple flap of a small box poked through the mess of used paper towels, soiled coffee filters and cigarette butts. He pushed the mess aside and pulled on the flap. When Jude saw that it was a box for a pregnancy test, he pulled it from the trash. The used test rattled in the box, and he pulled it out to examine it. He checked the lines carefully, double-checked the test with the images on the box. Jude glared through the window, thinking back to two months before when Molly had told him she was pregnant.

Kyle climbed from Molly's limp thighs when he finished, breathing heavily, and sat at the edge of the bed. He pulled his inhaler from the stack of *Guns & Ammo* magazine and shot two cold puffs of shampoo-tasting relief into his lungs. The police academy wouldn't take Kyle because of his asthma, so he'd settled for becoming a volunteer fire-fighter. He was doughy and soft, eager to please others despite the obvious dismissal most people offered him. Two weeks after Molly and Jude had arrived in Winton, she'd made a call to the fire department when she thought she smelled gas in the trailer. Kyle had lingered after the rest of the volunteers left, and he'd taken to Molly's sweet, toothy smile like iron shards to a magnet. Molly pulled a *Soldier of Fortune* magazine from the nightstand and flipped through the pages.

When Kyle caught his breath, he turned to her. "We should name it Patrick if it's a boy."

Molly ignored him and tossed the magazine. "Jude's going to find out about us."

"Why won't you just leave him and live with me?"

"Because horrible things will happen."

Kyle stared at her breasts. "What kind of things?"

"I wanted to leave him before, Kyle. He's fucking crazy. That's why he moved us out here, so I couldn't leave him. You're going to have to do more than take me out of a tiny trailer and put me in a tiny apartment to protect me."

"What else can I do?"

Molly sat up and rested on her knees. She wrapped her arms around Kyle's neck. He pushed back into her breasts and felt a rush of heat in his face. "You know a lot about guns and stuff, right?" she asked.

Kyle nodded.

"Doesn't the VFW where Jude works get robbed every few months? Well, what if it got robbed when Jude was working? What if the robbery went bad and Jude got hurt? Then I'd be safe. We could take the money and get a nicer place, a bigger place."

"Well, how would we—wait. You want me to do it?"

"Why not? Nobody will suspect you. They'll think it was some meth-head or something. We can take the money and get out of this shithole town. All you have to do is lie in wait for the customers to leave, then get him before he locks up."

"You mean the money?"

"Yeah. Of course."

Kyle worked his mustache. "I don't know, Molly."

Molly pushed herself away from him. "What the fuck do you know, then, video games? It's a simple plan, Kyle. If you can't handle this, how are you going to handle a baby? Don't you have the balls to do anything more than talk shit to eleven-year-olds?"

Jude returned to the trailer after a few hours. He'd walked through the snow along the edge of the river behind the trailer until the pants he wore were sleeves of ice. The skin on his calves burned where they'd rubbed against his frozen jeans. He scratched the thin tendrils of ice at the corners of his eyes. Molly pulled her wet hair to one side of her head and leaned over the stove to light a cigarette.

"You get out early, again?" she asked, sucking on the filter of the cigarette to get the cherry going.

"Early night for the town drunks," he answered.

"What'd you make tonight, thirty bucks?"

"Roughly." Jude worked his toes in his boots, silently begging for the feeling to come back to them.

"I'm almost out of cigarettes."

"You shouldn't be smoking those. You know, with the baby and all."

Molly looked down at his chest and crossed her arms. She ashed her cigarette over her shoulder into the sink. "I shouldn't be living in this shithole, either," she mumbled.

"Did you go anywhere today?" he asked.

"Yeah. Over the river and through the woods."

"Maybe next time you won't find your way back."

"I think the same thing every time you leave."

"Then who would pay your rent?"

"I don't know, maybe a real man."

Jude shook his head and slid his boots off. "Any hot water left?"

She smirked and blew a thin stream of smoke toward the ceiling.

Jude was a frigid, breakable piece of flesh when he lunged from the icy spray of the shower after just a minute or two. Soap still lingered on the backs of his hands and knees, on his shoulders and cheekbones. The only towel in the bathroom was damp from Molly's shower. He yanked at it, snapping the plastic hook from the wall. Jude dried himself, taking turns pressing his feet over the heating vent. Frost formed on the thin window next to the mirror, and in the thin steam of the room, he felt his anger rising. His skin flushed with warmth as his heart pounded and he twisted water from the towel. His jaw ached, his rage trading places with the pain of the cold. He tried to slow his breathing but couldn't. Being fired, all the times he'd bitten his tongue at the VFW, and now Molly's deceit. Jude pushed the knuckles of his fist together and shifted the weight on his feet, waiting to charge out of the bathroom—a slobbering mad-dog trotting up the center of the street, ready to shake the bones from road kill.

He remained in the bathroom until the anger passed.

Long after Molly had gone to sleep, Jude continued to pace the trailer. The structure felt flimsy as the wind buffaloed the walls, and Jude, reaching for balance in the things that had happened, slipped his hand into his pocket and counted his money again, wondering how far it could get him.

Molly woke to the sound of Jude leaving. She watched him walk down the street the way she did every morning or afternoon, then scrambled through the house, packing what few things she'd acquired since they'd arrived in Winton.

She started off with the basics, the dollar-store cosmetics and toiletries that had been a priority after their hasty arrival. She stared into the backpack she'd started packing, in at the cracked pink compact and tubes of lipstick and nail polish. Then, she dumped them in the sink, a habit that Jude had given up complaining about. She realized she didn't need any of those things.

Jude had acquired fewer things than she had, but the things he had were certainly more novel. He had a small pile of clothes folded on an antique trunk that he had dragged away from a yard sale. She remembered being slightly impressed with his haggling when he'd bought it. But more than that, she was jealous. She'd wanted it to be hers as soon as she heard Jude talking to the owner. She asked him for it, and it was the only time that she could remember when Jude had told her no. She emptied the trunk of its contents: a few books and a couple of tattered shirts Jude had asked her to sew for him. Molly finished her pillage through the trailer and called Kyle.

* * *

By the time Jude made it to town, the temperature had dropped ten degrees. The yellow convenience store that sold little but gas to motorists on their way south to Boston or north to the edge of Canada served as a bus station—a metal Greyhound sign hung above the door, faded and rusted at the edges. He bought a ticket to Birmingham, Alabama, a forty-hour trip that would push him closer and closer to someplace warmer. He had a cousin there who had promised him work anytime he needed it. With few options and little money, Jude settled for the prospect of washing dishes. At least the water would be warm. And even that didn't really matter. He'd found a job and a place to live in half a day when they arrived in Winton. He'd be fine. He'd move on. Rebuild. Forget.

The bus wouldn't leave until late, and the burly, pale-faced woman who sold him the ticket warned him that there was a possibility of delay due to the storm approaching. One more blizzard. One long, slow-moving trip to something warmer. Jude thought briefly of Molly, and with an effort to avoid spending the next several hours being angry, he forced himself to think of something else. Anger, temper, rage, aggression, violence and spite had never been present in his life. He had never loved anyone either. He'd said the words, but it seemed whenever he did, things changed. Speaking them, allowing them to push out into the air, made him realize that he was a liar—or would be. He hadn't realized that until Molly. Maybe that's why he took to Molly, because he was no different. She lied because the truth, like his declarations of love, were simply the whispers of all the ways they'd failed or were going to. Things like that kept people going in circles until the realization was too heavy to carry, and he refused to collapse under that weight.

Jude walked across the street to the Salvation Army Center. When he entered, the stale fabric smell—wet clothes dried in a basement—emitted from the racks of clothes and reminded him of the first time he and Molly walked into the trailer. Jude made his way to the small rack of books toward the back corner of the store. The smell began to make him queasy.

Most of the books were tattered romance novels and religious, God-finding, self-help bullshit that Jude found no interest in. The books, hardcover to paperback, like the clothing on the racks, were shelved by color, which forced Jude to scan the spines of them longer. He took the first three books of interest to him. He paid and went into the laundromat next to the Greyhound station, eager to get into the pages of one of them and forget about Molly.

Molly skipped through the house with excitement after she got off the phone with Kyle. Later that night, she'd take the money and leave Kyle there in the trailer. She'd take his truck and drive, get a few hours away before he realized she was gone. She'd stay in a hotel somewhere, with plush comforters and starched, thousand-thread-count sheets. There would be room service and endless hot water for showers. She'd wrap herself in a thick white robe and smoke cigarettes on the balcony and stare down at the homeless people near the grates where steam rose. The dress that she would buy would be expensive, from a store she'd never been to, and she'd have drinks at the hotel bar and find some miserable chump who wanted to forget, for one night, that he loved his wife.

She discovered a half-full pack of cigarettes behind the sofa. In the fridge, there were still four tallboy PBRs, and beneath the sink, she found a jug of Paisano with a little over a glass left and a nearly full bottle of triple sec that Jude had lifted from the VFW, mistaking it for tequila. She set the wine and liquor on the table and emptied the ashtray into the sink. She ran the water and watched it mix with the ash to form a silty pool in the drain stop. She lit a cigarette and smiled at the thought of Jude's reaction when he saw it. Then she realized that he wouldn't.

Molly winced away her smile with the thought of Kyle moving through the VFW with his gun. She went to the table and lit a cigarette and started on the wine. Vinegar. She choked down the tartness in gulps from a plastic cup and moved to the beer. The crisp pop of the tab was still resonating in the kitchen as she gulped it down, flushing the sour taste from her mouth. She opened the bottle of triple sec and took a pull from the bottle. The faint hint of orange brushed against her tongue. She alternated between gulps of beer and shots of triple sec. Outside, the snow fell thicker.

Molly lost track of time, found herself wavering through the house, out of beer, the cans scattered in chaos on the floor near the trash can. She took the last remaining swallows of the low-proof liquor and cast the bottle onto the couch where it bounced and fell to the carpet. Kyle would be there soon. She lifted the trunk, struggling with its heft, and put it down to adjust her grip. Again, she lifted and pushed through the aluminum door leading outside. She put the trunk down against the skirt of the trailer beneath the awning at the bottom of the steps. For a few moments, she marveled at her own cleverness. She wouldn't have been able to get the trunk outside in the night without waking Kyle. Then, she realized she could have had him load it in the truck for her. The few steps she took put a layer of sweat against her skin. She coughed and felt her heartbeat. The snow fell faster, and a wind came, cloaking her with a crisp relief. A gust forced her to shiver against the warmth she felt from the alcohol. When she turned toward the house, away from the gust of wind, the trailer door slammed shut.

Jude was halfway through his book when the bus pulled in front of the store. He pushed the paperback into his pocket and pulled out his strand of tickets. The driver stepped off. Jude handed the man his pass.

"All the way to Alabama," the driver said. His body bulged under the dark uniform and nylon jacket. "It's going to take us a while to get to Boston, but the heat's working real good tonight. No bags?"

Jude shook his head.

"Travel light. Good plan. Like I said, be slow goin' tonight. Get comfortable," he said, blinking snowflakes from his lashes. "After you, sir." The driver handed the remaining tickets back to Jude and extended his hand toward the door of the bus.

Jude climbed on, moving by the few sleeping passengers. He moved toward the back of the bus, until the smell of the bathroom toilet sanitizer made him stop and take a seat next to a woman wrapped in her jacket with her head resting against the window. She stared out at the falling snow. Jude settled into his seat and pulled the book from his pocket. The bus hissed and pulled forward.

* * *

Molly yanked on the door. The sturdiest part of the trailer was that door and Molly, having locked herself out before, knew she couldn't budge it. She hopped down the steps and ran to the back door of the trailer. The snow packed into her shoes and a few steps from the door, she fell. The bare skin on her arms and hands burned against the snow clinging to it. She got up and went to the back door that was bolted and held more firmly than the front. She went back to the front of the trailer and looked down the hill. Kyle would be there soon, she reminded herself. She scurried to the trunk, rifled through it, casting aside the things she'd packed it with, and pulled out the thin, wool blanket at the bottom. It was cold and stiff as she wrapped it around her shoulders, but it shelled her in a brief warmth that she was grateful for. She looked down the sides of the trailer at the windows, like tightly shut gills on a fish. Even if she could reach them and somehow get them opened, she wouldn't be able to fit through them, except for one. She fumbled through the snow toward the bathroom window.

The bathroom light was on and the window was unlocked. She went back to the front of the house and dragged the trunk through the snow to the window. The window was within reach if she stood on the trunk. She cupped her hands and warmed them, then placed them on the window and pushed up.

Nothing.

Goddamnit.

The edges of the window were lined with ice where the steam and moisture had seeped through and frozen. More cursing. Just beyond a thin piece of glass was the warmth she needed, and she couldn't find a way to get there. She struck the ice against the edges of the window with the bottom of her fist. Then again. And again. Bits of ice broke away. She worked the other side, hitting faster and harder. She hit too close to the glass and the window shattered, leaving jagged bits of glass in the frame. A heave of warm air pushed against her face. She reached up to pull a piece of glass. She could smell the damp towels and mildew of the bathroom. She yanked the first piece out like a tooth and as she motioned her arm to toss it aside, her footing on the trunk slipped. She grabbed for the window, her palms gouged by the jagged glass still in the pane, and fell. The trunk broke under her weight and she rolled from the snow and broken wood. Blood coursed over her fingers and fell against the snow where it was quickly buried by more.

Kyle pulled the slide release back on the AR-15. The bullet clamored into the chamber like a hard-struck billiard ball into a pocket. His breath blew out in short bursts. The blinds on the windows were still open and he could see a few of the patrons were still at the card table. He wondered if Molly had been mistaken when the bar closed. The more he thought, the more he lost his edge, the more he wanted to start his truck and drive home, the more he realized how much ridicule Molly would push down on him. He pulled the ski mask down over his face and got out of the truck.

The crunch of ice under his feet only seemed louder the slower he tried to walk toward the side entrance, where there was less light, where he could creep into the hallway and surprise the patrons. When he got to the steel door, his heart was racing. His breath came in short bursts and he wheezed. He stepped into the hallway on the outside of the bar that led to the restrooms. The patrons, a few scattered men who had just finished their card game, moved to the bar to finish their drinks. Kyle sputtered, he couldn't breathe. He thought of all those shootings at daycare centers and schools and movie theaters, and he couldn't understand the desensitization. He lost his breath and fumbled through his pockets.

Kyle stripped the ski mask over his head and took two solid puffs from his inhaler. Calm pushed through his lungs and he took another puff. He could feel his lungs open and ease into normal. The door from the hallway to the bar opened quietly and Kyle didn't notice its movement until the door had tapped his elbow. A red-mustached man with a cleft palate stared at him. His black-green plaid shirt was tucked into his jeans. The soft, worn leather of his boots matched his belt. Kyle looked up at him, lowering the inhaler from his mouth.

"What the hell are you doing?"

"I-I—"

"All the guns were supposed to be here by seven. The show isn't until tomorrow." The man sighed. "I'll get Linda."

The man walked back into the bar, calling for Linda. Kyle attempted to gather himself, remind himself of why he was there. He reached for the rifle and the door opened again.

The heavy woman entered the hallway. "Here to check your gun, huh? Should have been here by seven. Follow me."

She turned, shaking a set of keys in her hand, and went to a steel door that led to the basement. She unlocked it and pulled it open. Kyle stared at her, the gun balanced in his left hand. The flash of his video games pushed through his thoughts, the surrealistic cartoons of crashing automobiles and soldiers scrambling to objectives, subdued automatic gunfire and the bursts of blood and grunts of dying enemies became less real for him. Laughter came from the bar.

"You coming?" Linda asked.

"Jude? Is he working?"

"Jude is no longer with us. I have to get this place locked up, so if you want to check your gun, we'd better do it. The security detail will be here soon."

Kyle shook his head, thinking of Molly, how she was stuck in that crummy trailer with Jude. He looked down at the rifle. He knew what he had to do for Molly, for the baby.

"Actually, I'm having second thoughts. Can I come back tomorrow?"

Linda pushed the door closed and made no effort to hide her annoyance. "Sure. I'll lock the door behind you."

She pointed to the entrance Kyle had come through and he walked quickly outside, into the cold, where the snow fell like a tight, mesh net. A patch of ice at the bottom of the steps took his balance. He tumbled, tensing his hands around the rifle, hitting the trigger and the rifle fired. Bar stools pushed over the floor inside. He scrambled to his truck, spotting the shattered passenger-side headlight before he got in, and jerked the truck from the parking spot.

The broken headlight made it hard for him to see the edge of the road. His high beams only made it harder to see through the falling snow. He had to get to Molly. He had to get her out of there. He hunched over the wheel, wanting to drive faster but knowing he was already going too fast.

Enough time had passed for her teeth to chatter despite her attempts to clench her jaw. Headlights cut through the snow down on the road and she stood, pressing her thighs together, feeling the stiffness of her jeans on the thin skin around her knees. Thank Christ, she whispered, and the vehicle kept moving, passing the driveway. She pushed her hand out into the falling snow to wave, tried to yell, but they wouldn't have seen or heard her. Tears came and froze halfway down her cheeks like jeweled orbs that would sparkle and shimmer in the light if there had been any. She curled her arm back beneath the blanket, watching it like a slow-moving animal, no longer able to feel the cold at her fingertips.

Molly started down the driveway. Her eyelids stuck, frozen briefly as she blinked. The wind blew waves of snow around her, and in the depth of snow that she walked through, she could no longer tell if she was shambling down the drive, only that she was going downhill. The burning in her face was gone and her skin was numb. The ache in her toes, too, was gone and the gash in her hand felt like nothing more than her grip around a piece of rope. When the ground leveled off, she spotted the telephone pole at the end of the driveway, a few yards to her left. Beyond that, she saw the dim glow of a single light. Eagerness swept over her and she dragged her feet through the snow toward it, feeling her guts warm as it got closer. She did her best to trot, letting the blanket fall from her shoulder as she waved through the dropping snow. She laughed and forgot about how cold she was, exhilarated by the hope of salvation, warmth, comfort. The light was close. So close.

The rear of his truck pushed toward the center of the road and he slowed and corrected. It pushed toward the shoulder and he corrected again, that time too much. The crunch against the bumper jolted his arms and the broken post and mailbox he hit toppled over the hood. He gained control and continued on. He kept the truck close to the shoulder, bouncing as he hit mounds of snow. The single headlight offered a slight glimmer of guidance to Molly. A little farther along, another jolt, softer though than the first, but he watched for another mailbox. There was nothing but snow on the hood, melting from the heat of his engine, and he let off the gas to turn up the driveway.

The impact forced her sudden exhale, a violent hiccup. She heard the metal cough through the hiss of snowfall, felt the weightlessness and breeze against her skin as she tumbled, spinning into the depth of snow on the banking in a sprawl. Warmth rushed to her eyes and ears, flushed through her cheeks and over her chest, down the insides of her ribs and spine like a hot breath. She watched the snow swirl around the taillights as they turned up the driveway, watched them fade and fold away into the night.

DELIVERY MAN

Earl sits in a stool, staring at a divot in the lacquered, wooden bar as if he's alone in the room. He ignores me when I take a seat next to him. To Earl, I'm just a stranger. He smells of must and wet cardboard. Earl taps his shot glass against the bottle of rye. Mike, the bartender, grabs the bottle and pours another shot for Earl, who lifts the glass and rolls the shot down his throat.

The news comes on the small television in the corner above the liquor shelf. It's the same story they showed an hour before, and an hour before that, that they'll show an hour from now. Eight years running, someone's been killing folks on Christmas day.

Mike points a toothpick at Earl. "Better watch out for this one. You're a sure victim for this guy."

"A guy like me?"

"Low-life fuckin' degenerate, what else?"

Mike laughs. Earl takes a pull off his beer and stuffs the bottle into his jacket pocket. "Hand me another one for the road."

Mike pulls a Bud from the cooler and slides it across the

bar. "What time you coming over tomorrow?"

Earl starts for the exit. "I have shit to do tomorrow," he says, pulling the door open and letting a heave of cold air surge through the room.

"It's Christmas. What do you have to do on Christmas?"

"Fuck Christmas," Earl calls out from beyond the door that's already closed.

Mike looks at me. "Almost last call. You want another one?"

I nod. He grabs me a beer, and I slide my money across the bar.

"That one's on me, little lady. Merry Christmas." He puts a shot glass in front of me. "Some daily bread," he says as he pours it.

"Lead us not into temptation," I mutter.

He gives me a wink and goes to the door to draw the shade. He steps back behind the bar and begins his close-out routine. I sit quietly, sip on the whiskey, watch the snow whirl beyond the rectangular window above the door. Mike kills the lights outside and I can't see the snow anymore. In the bar, we sit in the gloom while drops of melted snow drip from my boots to the floor.

The next morning, I clear the snow from the windshield and the mirrors of my delivery truck. It's a half-day of work, but it's still a busy day. I carry packages to houses, heavy things in small boxes, watch the excitement on people's faces as they call to whomever else is in the house that the delivery man is here. They always say that, *delivery man*. They don't look at me, just the package. They don't look at me even when they sign.

I turn on the radio, try to find a station playing music instead of commentary on the *Christmas Killer*. Each station buzzes with past stories, excitement, hope that the twelve-bullet victim will turn up. They talk the same way the people I deliver packages to: eager, vibrant about what they're receiving, ignoring the reason for the season. The DJs take calls from fans disappointed that the Christmas Killer hasn't delivered.

The last delivery takes me to the edge of town, to a trailer that's banked with snow. It's the lightest package I've delivered. The truck parked in the driveway is sideways and I notice the stretch of ice in front of the house. I park the van and walk carefully over the ice. I step up to the porch, notice the small pool of frozen blood on the top step, the broken pieces of glass from a beer bottle. There's a torn glove off to the side. My heart pounds as I rap on the door. When Earl answers, he shakes his head and takes the box. His right hand is bandaged with a strip of cloth torn from a green flannel shirt.

"Who sent me a package?"

"The ghost of Christmas past," I tell him, and my voice cuts through the tight wind the way I pack my Christmas spirit—snug, pushed into brass cylinders, tucked neatly in six chambers, ready to deliver.

WOOD FOR THE FIRE

Adam could feel the body heat from the man who sat in the chair before him rising into his clothes. He felt the contour of the other body in the soft fabric, the grooves the man's weight left at the edge of the seat and in the armrests. Adam's fat-fingered ghost handprint faded from the edge of the stage, where he'd leaned forward for the girl who just walked off—Persephone. He settled in the seat and waited for her to come back. They always came back. There was something he thought he recognized about her. The dim light did that sometimes, made men think the women on the stage were someone from their past, someone they loved or damaged.

He could smell the starchy scent of new bills as they wafted through the smoke onto the stage, like flakes of ash sifting through a fire. He smelled sweat and the sticky-mouthed breath of the girls who panted through the last part of their dance. But Persephone didn't pant. Adam wanted to see her last dance. That's the one he heard so much about.

Persephone watched Adam from the back of the room, saw him settle a little more in his seat with each girl. She stayed close to the corner, out of the stream of the black lights that seared white into the darkness of the space around them where other men slumped in seats hoping for some attention they couldn't find outside. She waited there, watching the other girls slide onto Adam's lap. She could smell him, his scent lingered from when they'd met before. It filled her nose like something burning on cast iron. The girl on his lap looked over his shoulder for someone else to approach as he talked.

When Persephone got back to the stage, Adam was still there. She gripped the pole as she marched out, lifted her weight and spun. That's all she wanted to do, spin until the dim light faded to nothing and she could finally be alone, feel something warm instead of the cold that surrounded her whenever she thought about touching a man. The smoke machine pushed out more gray between the lyrics and she let her focus drift and glide with the music. Adam leaned forward in his chair. His lips parted slightly. His hands found the edge of the stage. She'd waited a while for his attention.

The music started to fade again, and Persephone strutted to the end of the stage with the bottle of 151 and took a swig. The song went silent, the smoke machine hissed and the room went dark. A click came from the stage, sang through the darkness, and a light flickered there in the dark. Persephone's face moved toward the light in her hand, and she blew a flame into the air above Adam, saw his cold eyes catch the fire. In the back of the room, another man sat and watched the stage. He huddled beneath the shadow of a baseball cap. He kept his fingers interlocked except for his index fingers that he kept in a steeple covering his lips. He'd found her.

* * *

Erin married Phillip young, and the only thing they knew was an indifference to the struggles they were promised for their future. Then, they learned about tension and distance, economic struggle, rising interest rates and insurance deductibles, student loan repayments and credit scores, miscarriages and endless fertility appointments and consultations. They lost their place somewhere in their shuffling among the things they had to deal with and couldn't remember the way back to where they were before, when they went to bed together at night and shared breakfast in the morning. The things they couldn't control became the motivation to find a way to argue about the things they could, habits that they'd ignored when they were busy in the bliss of their marriage.

She suggested the outfit one night before she went to bed when she found him at the kitchen table with a glass of whiskey, his shirt unbuttoned after another disappointing day on the sales floor. He left the whiskey there and followed her to bed.

She bought the outfit the next day, and when Phillip rushed into the house that afternoon, she delighted in the spark that had brought them back to the warmth of their marriage. Phillip suggested the car, and they both forgot about pointing knives down in the dish rack and milk in the refrigerator door.

In the driveway, he opened the door for her, and she slid her finger along his waistband just under his belt as she climbed into the seat. Phillip moved around the car and got in, his hand resting on the door handle as he stared at her legs, how they crossed at the knee, and the hem of her white leather mini-skirt pressed into her skin. He sat there for a while, staring, his smile growing as he followed the edge of her shin down to the heels she wore. He shut his door and looked at his wife's face, the nervous smile, her eyes darting over his expression.

"I'm—" He paused, biting off his words. "I love you," he told her, and those words, too, found their place again between them where *I'm sorry* would have lingered.

They drove for an hour in silence. Their hands had joined before Phillip had pulled from the driveway. Each of them took in the landscape of their town, the changes lining the sidewalk like someplace new and dangerous— the first, lustful tug on the waistband of a stranger's jeans. She thought about how easy it was for them to find this place again, the quiet, a form of happiness and comfort. She muddled over disappointment that they hadn't gotten there sooner, that they let themselves get mired in a distance between each other.

When Phillip slowed and stopped at a red light, she asked him, "What do you want for breakfast tomorrow?"

"I want you in sweatpants and one of my button-downs. I want to stay in bed. I want to call out of work on Monday. I want to forget the past six months." He turned to her. "I want you to love me again."

He looked back through the windshield and waited for the light.

"Phillip."

"Yeah?"

"I still love you."

He lifted her hand and kissed her knuckles.

Phillip drove to the south end of town, where there had once been a four-screen movie theater, a building now abandoned, boarded and draped with graffiti, the last holdout of a piece of the town that they remembered. There had been a small convenience store in front of the theater, where they'd go to buy candy instead of purchasing what the theater offered. The carpet in there had smelled like urine, and the store itself was only slightly bigger than a walk-in closet. They'd gone there for their first date back in high school, and nostalgia, like most things, was the landmark they needed. Phillip parked near the rusted chain-link fence that leaned toward the steep hill sloping down to the river.

He parked facing the sun, and they watched as it sunk behind the taller buildings to the west, the hotels that had been built in anticipation of the casinos that elevated the small town to a status of something else, something that didn't seem to fit it, like sleeves that were too short. The sky dimmed, and Erin leaned toward him and rested the side of her face on his shoulder.

Phillip worked his thumb gently against the inside of her knee, moving in small circles as the sun set then worked his way up her thigh. She parted her legs and extended one foot to rest her heel against the corner of the dash. Phillip hadn't touched her that way for months. Their moments of affection had been pecks and skin grazes as they passed each other. There had been nothing intentional until then. Erin's breathing shifted, slower, and she closed her eyes. Phillip focused on her face, her teeth pushing against her bottom lip. They didn't hear the car roll to a stop behind them.

Persephone led Adam through the room, past the hidden glare of the man in the baseball cap, to the VIP booth, a darker room with dim lamps that hovered just behind the vinyl chairs. She motioned him to the chair and waited for him to get comfortable. As the music came on, a slow, somber melody that moved her slowly toward him. Adam pinched the knees of his pant legs and pulled the slack bunching against his inner thighs. As his hands withdrew, she dropped to her knees in front of him and slapped his quads, her head hanging toward the floor and her shoulder blades pointing sharply toward the ceiling. She threw her head back. Strands of the blond wig wisped against his chin and the tip of his nose. She pushed his legs together and straddled him, pushing her knees into the corner of the chair on either side of his hips.

She pushed her tits over his face, took a grip of his hair and jerked his head back. She stroked his cheek with her tongue.

"You like it rough, don't you, darling?" he whispered.

She palmed his mouth, "I'm nobody's darlin'."

She pushed away from him to her feet and turned, bending over to reach between her legs and spread his knees. She gripped the armrests and sunk against him, pushing and wedging her ass between his legs. Then, she moved slowly, circling her hips. His hand slid up her ribs and she rotated to slap his wrist. She grabbed his face, squeezing his cheeks hard against his teeth.

"Don't. Fucking. Touch."

Adam held his hands up, casting finger shadows over her body. She swung her leg over his head and landed her heel against the armrest. She pulled the card from her bustier and wrapped her arms around his head to push his face against her chest.

"If you want to touch, meet me here. Room 437. Two

hours." She pushed his head away and slipped the card inside his shirt collar.

She turned and walked toward the door. When she opened it, the flash of the strobe light came into the VIP and he squinted against the sudden light. She reached back to close the door and he saw it, the small seahorse tattoo along the edge of her breast, and he remembered where he'd met her.

Erin hit the rearview mirror with her forehead when she sprang forward after the knock on the glass. Phillip looked up at the window toward the bright beam of the flashlight that shined in. He saw the dark, drab color of the police uniform, the glint of the badge.

"Step out of the car."

Erin huddled in the seat, a flash of embarrassment heating her face. Phillip got out.

"Put your hands against the vehicle."

"Look, officer. This is a misunderstanding. My—"

Phillip felt the thrust forward before he realized the cop had grabbed him. He spun and landed with his chest against the trunk of the car. The cop patted down his pant legs around his stomach and down his arms. He brought Phillip's right hand to the small of his back and cuffed it. He cuffed the left.

"Officer, please. I haven't done anything wrong."

Erin climbed from the car.

The cop squeezed Phillip's shoulder and pointed at her. "Get back in the vehicle. Get back in the fucking vehicle, right now."

Erin sunk back into her seat and closed the door.

The cop pulled the contents of Phillip's pockets and tossed them onto the trunk of the cruiser—change, the pocket knife his grandfather had given him, a ballpoint pen, the small notebook he kept in his back left pocket to even out the wallet he carried in his right. Then there was the chapstick container and inside it was the stale joint that Phillip had been saving. The cop pulled it out and put it to his nose.

"What's this for?"

Phillip shrugged, half hoping that the night would move faster, that he could get it all over with and get into bed with his wife and wrap his arms over her ribs and grip her shoulder before he fell asleep—the way he used to get to sleep every night. He wanted to forget all the things that had built between them.

"Officer, it's just a joint. I wasn't even going to smoke it."

The cop nodded. "And the hooker? I suppose you weren't going to do that either."

"What? Hooker? That's my wife. She's not a—"

"Sure, buddy. Let's go."

The cop grabbed Phillip's arm and pulled him toward the cruiser. Phillip pulled his arm away.

"This is ridiculous. This is not what you think it is."

The cop slammed his open hand against the back of Phillip's neck. He dug his fingers into the tender spot of his bicep just above the elbow and marched Phillip to the cruiser. He opened the back door and pushed Phillip inside.

The cop stalked toward Erin and opened her door. "What's a pretty thing like you go for?"

"What are you talking about?"

"Yeah. Be that way." He took her arm and pulled her

from the car.

"Phillip," she yelped.

"This one's on him."

Persephone left through the back entrance of the club and tapped the bouncer on his shoulder as she passed. Phillip stood beneath the street light at the corner where he was illuminated by the flickering light, the baseball cap lifted slightly. The swarm of moths and other insects gave the ground a chandelier effect. For a moment, she took in the sweet-sixteen moment, the fantasies, fairy tales and other lies she'd learned as a child, her knight in shining armor standing there for the chance to rescue her from doom. What she didn't realize as a child was that the knight's armor is tarnished, and the dragons are more careful where they breathe fire. She thought about walking the other way, but she adjusted the strap of her backpack on her shoulder and approached him. She stayed a few feet from the edge of the light, and Phillip flicked his cigarette behind him and walked toward her.

"When did you start smoking again?"

"When you left."

"You shouldn't be here. I told you not to look for me."

"Well, a husband usually likes to know what his wife's been doing for the past four months."

"I'm not your wife anymore."

"Is that really what you want?"

"Why are you here, Phillip?"

"I want you to come home. You don't belong here, in this place, taking men into back rooms. Is this a coping mechanism or something?"

"A coping mechanism?"

"How is this helping you?"

"Go home, Phillip."

She turned and walked away. The bouncer took a few steps from the door to watch Phillip. Phillip gathered the lingering echoes of her footsteps as she turned the corner of the building. He walked back to the parking lot where he'd parked and unlocked the door of his car. He got in and drove home.

When he got home, Phillip wandered through the house. From boredom or habit, he went to the refrigerator and peered inside. The light struck through the room and Phillip closed the door. He went to the couch in the living room and pushed the blankets and the pillow to the side. He slumped against the cushions and stared into the branches outside the living room window. The streetlight cast a shadow of them across the floor of the open room. He slammed the pillow against the armrest of the couch and pulled the blanket over his legs as he reclined. It felt like he'd slept for hours when the shadow broke the light from outside. A small smile spread across his face as he pulled from his dream of Erin and opened his eyes to the presence in the room.

Phillip's face was smeared with tears and spit where he pressed against the glass in the back seat of the police cruiser. His throat burned from his previous screams and his voice was gone, torched. Blood dried in the spaces between his fingers from the cuts on his wrist. One of the handcuffs had severed a tendon in his struggle. He toppled out to the ground when the cop opened the door. "Today's your lucky day," the cop whispered as he unlocked Phillip's handcuffs. "I'd get her out of here, though. I wouldn't want you to get picked up for soliciting."

Phillip held his arms at his side against the ground. He tasted the sand and rubbed the broken piece of glass from his lip with his tongue. The tires of the police cruiser backed away, inches from his face, and Phillip pushed himself to his knees. He rose, staggered over to the car and looked inside.

Erin had curled herself into a ball on the back seat. Her makeup ran in black tendrils over her nose. Her eyes watered and stayed fixed on the space in front of her, the seam on the back of the driver's seat. The heel of her right shoe was broken, the other on the ground beside the door. The fabric of her top was torn, and her bra, the seahorse tattoo on her breast exposed. He reached down to touch her calf and she pulled her leg away. He stripped his suit jacket and draped it over her. The night seemed to sigh around him, that *what did you expect* kind of sigh that his father often offered him as a child whenever he hurt himself, that merciless, authoritative indifference that people held when something awful wasn't happening to them.

Phillip drove quickly through town, and when he stopped, he looked into the back seat. "Let's go," he told her.

She turned her head slowly, squinted at the sight in front of her and the expectation she had to be home. She jerked upright and pushed herself against the seat, cowering from the light of the sign for the police department. Her jaw quivered.

"Jesus, I'm sorry. I'm sorry." He drove them home.

She sat in the corner of the bathroom while the shower ran and the steam slowly filled the small room. Condensation spread over the porcelain of the toilet and she noticed the cardboard sleeve of an empty toilet paper roll. She looked around the room at the toothpaste cap, the unscrewed top of the mouthwash bottle, the small mound of the clothes she'd had on before she put on the outfit clumped on top of the wicker hamper, all the things Phillip hated, things they'd argued about.

Phillip sat at the edge of the bed and watched the wafting steam present movement under the corner of the door through the strip of light beneath it. He listened for her movement, her entry into the shower, but it was just the echo of water in the shower stall. He waited for a long time, then stood and walked to the door. He lifted his hand, folded his fingers to rap his knuckles against the barrier and looked at the blood drying on his wrist. He felt the pain there for the first time. The question he was going to ask, the string of words on his tongue backed him away from the door.

She was not okay.

He woke as the sun came through the bedroom windows. He was on his side, his feet still touching the floor, and he bolted upright. The bathroom door was ajar and the shower was still running. He stood and stepped over to the door, glancing through the crack for her. He felt the chill of the water in the room. He entered, opened the shower stall and turned off the water.

He found her outside in the middle of the backyard, smoke from the fire she'd lit purging over her.

Phillip went to the police, without her, two days later, when Erin refused to come out of the nursery, when he felt that his quiet footsteps on the carpet were too loud. When he walked up to the glass cubby and the silver metal screen that he was supposed to speak through, he saw that there was a cop on the other side. How did he tell the cop there he wanted to file a complaint? Was that what he was supposed to say?

"Can I help you?" The cop's soft, boyish voice came through the screen.

"Yeah, I need to talk with a supervisor about one of your officers?"

"Are you here to file a complaint?"

"Yes. I am."

"Have a seat. We'll be with you in a minute."

Phillip turned to the three metal folding chairs against the wall, the corner table with a stack of magazines, the pages torn and furled at the edges. Complaint? Is that all it was, just a complaint? It already seemed like a waste of time, but he couldn't do anything else. He couldn't keep tiptoeing around his house doing nothing while his wife shut herself away in a room.

More than two hours later, a buzz vibrated in the air of the room and the steel door beside the glass cubby clicked before it opened. Another police officer opened the door and held it with his foot.

"Are you here for the complaint?"

Phillip stood.

The cop looked him up and down, chewed the gum in his mouth with long, slow jaw strokes and waved Phillip on with a head movement. The cop led him to a small room halfway down the hallway to the right. Phillip saw a couple of cops in one of the rooms laughing as they slapped each other on the shoulder. Phillip's escort opened the door of a room labeled Conference Room 3.

"Wait here. Someone will be in in a second."

Phillip waited almost another hour.

A man in a suit came into the room. His shirt was wrinkled and the knot on his tie was loose. Phillip noticed how much the rest of the tie had faded in color except the knot. He didn't wear a badge or a gun, and Phillip wanted to ask who he was, but didn't. The man slapped a yellow legal pad on the table and a dropped a pen on top of that. He sat down and pointed to the matching chair across the table.

"Have a seat and tell me what you're here for."

Phillip told him the story. He felt his voice shaking the more the story progressed. The man across from him made notes and his eyes, for one brief moment, widened when Phillip told him about the officer moving toward Erin, what he'd done. Phillip finished the story.

"Explain to me what you were doing with the marijuana."

"What?"

"The marijuana. What was it for?"

"Is that really relevant?"

"Everything is relevant."

"I thought a rape would be more relevant than a misdemeanor charge for pot."

The man smirked and looked down at the bandages around Phillip's wrists. "What happened?" He asked, pointing at Phillip's hands with the end of his pen.

"The handcuffs."

"Can you describe anything about the officer?"

Phillip thought about the cops he saw when he walked in and realized any description he could offer described most of them. He gave as many details as he could.

"Alright. What was your wife wearing the night of the

attack?"

"What? Why does that have anything to do with this?"

"Well, the attacker could be targeting women based on what they're wearing."

"I already told you who the attacker was."

"No. You told me that the alleged attacker was a cop."

"My wife and I were on a date. What does it matter what she was wearing or if she was wearing anything at all?"

"It matters."

"If my house got robbed, would you ask me why I had anything of value in my home? I'm telling you a police officer raped my wife, and I want you to do something about it instead of sitting there writing doodles on your fucking piece of paper."

"Look, son. I know you're upset—"

"Upset? My wife's destroyed. I get the luxury of being upset."

"Son. I don't know the best way to tell you this, but it's very possible that the person who victimized your wife was impersonating a cop. It happens."

"I was put in a police cruiser. All of the equipment was in the front. It was a cop, not a fucking rapist impersonating one."

"You may have been in a police cruiser, but that doesn't mean the person driving it was a cop."

"How would someone get their hands on a police cruiser?"

"These kinds of people are clever. They could have taken one of the cruisers that was in for repairs."

"So, if people are impersonating cops, what are you doing about it?"

"Well, when we get a complaint that…"

"A complaint similar to someone telling you a cop raped their wife?"

"I know this can't help you now, but did you verify that the person who assaulted you was a police officer? Did you see a badge number or any identification?"

"I was busy being thrown against my car and handcuffed."

"Did you get a plate number?"

"No."

"I don't really know how to help you, son, except to file a report. Where does your wife stand on all of this?"

"She doesn't know I'm here."

"Well, if your wife was the one who was attacked, we'll need to hear from her."

"You want my wife to come into a police station where there are cops and one of them raped her?"

"This is very serious. If you want us to proceed with an investigation, we're going to need to start somewhere."

"Why don't you show me photos of the police officers, and I'll tell you which one did it."

"That's not how it works."

"Then how does it work? If she were just attacked by some random man and you had a series of photos of convicted rapists, then wouldn't you allow me to look at those?"

"Well, that would be different. Those are convicted rapists. This is a police officer that you're accusing. You've given me a description of a man that could fit seventy-five percent of the police officers we have here. And since your wife was the one who was attacked, she'll have to be the one to file the report."

Phillip stood and walked out.

When he got home, the living room furniture had been pushed against the walls. The same in the kitchen. The nursery door was locked, and if Erin was in there, she didn't answer.

He left things the way they were, and over the next couple weeks, tried to catch her when he heard her shuffling through the house. Her clients called, and he took messages and slid them under the door to the nursery. He made her dinner, and after a week, stopped leaving the plates by the door where they'd remain untouched. He continued to make food, but he'd leave the leftovers in the refrigerator. After work one day, he found her hair in a pile in their bedroom sink. In the nursery, he found her letter, and that was all that remained of her.

Persephone watched through the window of the hotel room, down toward the spot where the old movie theater once stood. It was just a flat space in the landscape now. Adam hadn't shown. She waited another hour, packed the things she'd put out and went home.

She latched down the two deadbolts after she slipped into her apartment—a small studio on the west end of town, the part of the town that dropped further into dilapidation after the new apartment complexes had been built along the river. She could see them before she'd painted the windows black when she moved in. There was no lease, and she'd convinced the manager to rent her the place without a background check and the other information essentials with an extra two hundred dollars each month, which was an easy bargain. Later, she discovered that it was exactly the type of place where anonymity reigned. Hookers, dealers, bookies and other sorts moved in and out of the building all the time. It was perfect for her. She'd done everything she could not to be found.

She used a sleeping bag and kept her backpack against the back wall when she slept. She'd sleep in her clothes, and the bathroom door had a deadbolt. She kept a small duffel bag for her laundry that she did once a week in the coin-op washing machine in the basement. Throughout the apartment, in the drawers and taped to doors, in each cabinet and in the cushions of the chair against the wall of the apartment, she'd stashed knives that she'd bought at various flea markets—all the same basic, full tang stainless steel blades that she'd spent a week sharpening.

She sat on her sleeping bag with her backpack and pulled her money from the interior pocket of the main pouch. Did she miss her chance? She thought about a new strategy while she counted her money. Maybe she'd leave town for a little while, come back for a new approach. Phillip entered her mind briefly, and she was making every attempt to push him from her mind when the knock came to her door. The memory of him had frustrated her, but now she was angry that he'd followed her there, to her home. She shoved the money back into her pack and went for the door.

When Phillip would leave for work, she'd stand in the open doorway of the nursery for several minutes to make sure he'd left. After, she'd go into the bedroom and curl against the pillow in the bed that still smelled like him. She'd listen to him when he came home, through the door of the room as he made dinner, doing his best to make as little noise as possible. She wanted to be in his arms, feel some comfort from him, and there were days that she stood in the living room, waiting for him to return. Then his car would pull in and she'd panic, she'd see him wrapping her up in his arms and she couldn't breathe, her stomach knotted, and she felt the gritty scrape inside her guts. Before he could open the door, she'd dart back to the nursery and huddle in the corner to catch her breath.

Saturday, three weeks after the night in the car, she set out to leave. She couldn't take the daily flex of anxiety that she felt when Phillip would sit by the door and talk to her, how it made her weep into a rolled-up T-shirt on the other side of the wall. She packed a bag and left him a note. She had to leave, move to some place where she was anonymous and alone, track her way back to herself somehow. She had the rental car pick her up at the house.

She was speeding when she got pulled over on the long stretch of wooded road toward the airport. The trembling in her hands made it difficult to put the car into park. Her breathing quickened, became shallow and she felt a curling sickness in her stomach that rolled upward toward her throat. The cop approached, and she struggled to lower the window a few inches.

"Ma'am, do you know why I pulled you over?"

He was younger, a boyish face and a proud smile, like he was strolling through an auditorium celebrating his success.

"I'm heading to the airport. I'm running a little late. I'm sorry, officer. I'll slow it down."

"I'm going to need to see your license, registration and proof of insurance."

She clenched her jaw and tried to compose her shaking

hands as she reached for the documents.

"Are you alright, ma'am?"

She pushed her lips together and nodded. *Ummhmmm.*

"Well, you're shaking quite a bit. Are you nervous about something?"

"Cops," she blurted, which made the officer twitch. She cleared her throat. "Sorry. Cops make me nervous." She found her license and the other papers and handed them through the window.

He took them. "I'll be right back." He took a step and paused. "Ma'am."

"Yeah?"

His smile returned. "There's no reason to be nervous. We're the good guys."

As he marched away, the passenger door of the cruiser opened. She adjusted the rearview with her index finger, trying to keep her movements minimal. She watched the cruiser, her right hand squeezing the shifter, her foot wavering on the brake, feather soft, ready to press the gas to the floor after she moved the shifter down. Another cop got out of the car. Her heart beat in a quick, throbbing tamp. Her eyes went blurry as she stared at the rearview. She squeezed them shut, blinked them back into focus. The cop sat against the hood of the cruiser, staring at the vehicle. When the driver got out, the two of them approached.

She kept her focus on the cop who'd gotten out of the passenger side. She told herself it couldn't be, had to be the uniform, but as he got closer, she realized it was him. Her eyes narrowed, and she gripped the wheel. He stopped at the rear bumper, looked into the car through the back window. It was him.

"Ma'am."

She gasped, catching her breath again and snapped her attention to the officer at her window.

"I'm going to let you go with a warning today. I need you to slow it down, though, alright?"

"Y-yes, sir."

He handed the papers and her ID back through the window. "You have a good day now."

"Officer."

"Yes, ma'am."

"I hope you don't mind my asking, but what are your names? I don't always meet cops I'd like to praise."

"Oh, I don't mind. I'm Officer Mitchell."

"And your partner?"

"That's my supervisor. That's Sergeant Wood."

She gave him a petty smile. "Thank you, Officer Mitchell. I appreciate that." She closed the window, checked her mirror and pulled onto the road.

Erin pulled the rental into the terminal and left the key in the ignition. She bypassed the booth to check-in the car and walked through the airport to the arrival corridor. She flagged a cab and got a ride to the library. She started there, gathering information, as much as she could, piling it in her mind.

Her focus on Sergeant Wood shifted the preoccupied thoughts that were there, the anxiety, the event itself. They didn't disappear, but they were tethered at such a distance, she found an ability to keep her mind moving in a straight direction, a goal, an ends. Her days became that, and that focus she found became her design. She followed Wood, adapting more and more each day. She traded sneakers for steel-toed Chippewas, her running capris for cargo pants, the zip-up windbreaker for a hoodie, and she wore a baseball cap the way that Phillip wore them, pulled down to her eyebrows to shadow her face.

The only consistency in Wood's schedule was Cherry's. A "gentleman's" club, the sign said, and that made her think about how easily men were defined. And Erin, through months of mentoring, learned how to hide everything about herself in the dark room of the club, where she could breathe, where she could lean at forty-five degrees against the stone and push forward. And in there, in the dark, she felt relief. It was a soothing comfort that men weren't allowed to touch her in there the way they had outside. After a few months, she found her edge. She found Persephone.

She snapped the deadbolts open, and as she turned the knob she realized that Phillip wasn't the only one who could have followed her. Gloved fingers wrapped around the edge of the door and his other gloved hand darted through the open space. She smelled it against the gloves, the heavy odor of sulfur, matches, gunpowder. The hand gripped the back of her neck and she met the door with her face. She heard the crack of her nose, the drilling pressure between her eyes and her balance went soft. He was in the apartment, re-bolting the deadbolts as she fell to the floor.

She rolled to her stomach and tried to shake off the dizziness.

"I knew you were a fucking whore. What were trying to do, get back at me?" He watched her from the door as he spoke. She rolled to a sitting position and scooted toward her sleeping bag. She inched her left hand beneath it and worked the handle of the knife into her palm.

Wood tilted his head at her effort and produced a sly grin. He moved toward her.

"What are you going to do, sweetheart, try to cut my dick off?"

She pulled the knife and showed him, pointed the tip at his face. He kept moving toward her. She squinted the watering in her eyes away. A few feet away from her, he lowered slightly into a crouch. He continued to move toward her, interlocked his fingers and worked his gloves tighter. He moved his shoulders from side to side, inching closer to her. He worked his fists in a circle. She held the knife, a feeble grip, and he opened his right hand and shook it at her then slapped the knife from her hand with his left.

She swung her right hand forward and buried a different blade in the contour of his hip. He dropped to a knee and she rolled to her back and thrust her heel into his jaw. He'd already grabbed for the gun in his belt, and it flipped through the air as she kicked him. She drew her leg back and rolled to the side, sliding into the chair against the wall in one fluid motion. She reached over the armrests of the chair and snatched two more blades taped to the bottom. Wood rolled to his stomach and reached for the gun; she lurched forward and drove a blade through his hand. The blade sliced through flesh and chipped through bone until it bit into the floor.

She pulled the pistol from beneath his middle finger that got to the gun before she'd pinned his hand to the floor. She stood back, pinched her nose and winced against the pain.

"Your dick's not worth the effort to find to cut off."

"You're going to pay for this."

She stepped over his chest and he snatched at the knife, catching a grip of her right wrist with his left hand. She dropped the blade, caught it with her left and slid the blade along the inside of his wrist, cutting deep, and his grip softened, and his fingers drooped, waving like fabric under water.

He curled his arm into his chest, wincing, trying to bite the pain away in the thin spaces between the grit of his teeth. He let out a subdued groan.

"Stop, please. I'm sorry. Fuck, don't cut me again. Just go ahead and get out of here. I won't say anything." He nudged his chin toward the door. "Go ahead. Come on."

She looked down on him, his blood coursing down his forearm and over his stomach. His leg quivered. The index finger of his right hand twitched against the carpet.

"Not yet."

She stepped over him and he started to chuckle to himself. "You fucking bitch. You're going to burn for this."

She pulled her backpack from the corner and pulled out the bottle.

"Funny you should say that."

She uncapped the 151 and dumped it over him as she circled his body.

"What the fuck are you—You crazy fucking bitch."

She pulled the flare from her back pocket, stripped the cap, and sparked it.

On her way out of the building, she pulled the fire alarm. She took the side entrance and cut through the small patch of forest toward the river, toward the walking path that connected both sides. At the crest of the walking bridge, she looked back on the complex, the people filtering out. Smoke billowed from the window she'd opened before she'd left. She slid the backpack from her shoulder and unzipped it. She dumped the contents into the rushing water below and let the pack drop to the water as well. She took a breath, the sun climbing into the horizon down the river, and walked toward home.

The furniture in the house was still where she'd left it, pushed against the walls. Phillip was on the couch, where he'd been sleeping since she left, hoping he'd wake in the night to her return. Tears welled in her eyes as she approached him. She felt the warmth of their home and tried to remember where the furniture had been. The sounds of the words she wanted to say were already trying to climb over her tongue. She smiled. *I still love you*, she'd tell him. She reached for his shoulder and noticed it then, the tapping sound on the carpet, his blood dripping over the couch, and in the dark saw the darker spot, the bullet hole in his temple.

WATCH

Ashley's ears were still ringing from the gunshot. Her wrists had begun to ache. That ache had traveled up the tendons and through the muscle in her forearms and nestled into a cramp just below her elbows. Her mouth was dry, and the subdued tears that had fallen over her face and streamed down her nose were drying at the corners of her lips. The room she sat in was cold, and just as she realized the discomfort of the room, a body shiver rattled the links of the chains on her handcuffs against the wooden chair she sat in.

The room was an oversized cubicle with beige walls and a plain, wood veneer table that had been watermarked in the center with soda cans and coffee mugs. There was a chair opposite her, cushioned leather, comfortable. In the corner, legal pads and a box of black pens, the cheap kind that office supply stores sold in bulk, were stacked on top of a two-drawer filing cabinet next to a box of tissues. There was a door behind her, and when it opened, she corrected her posture.

"Take those cuffs off," a woman's voice commanded.

Ashley felt a set of meaty hands grip her wrist while the

woman carrying a file folder and a small box walked around the table and sat in the comfortable chair. The handcuff clicked, and her left arm was free. The hands took hold of her right arm and freed the other cuff. Ashley massaged the tender bones in her wrists and felt a draft sneak through the sleeves of her shirt. The woman placed the file folder on the table between them, inched it into perfect position at the corner. The woman did the same with the box she carried at the other corner.

The door closed, and Ashley focused on the woman in front of her. The crow's feet at the corners of her eyes looked like the stems of a gem-set for the blue that peered back at her. The woman's mocha skin spilled into the fuchsia button-down she wore. She grabbed the box of tissues and held it out for Ashley. Ashley took one and wiped the salty residue from the corners of her mouth and eyes.

The woman smiled, her teeth showing through a grin that had parted and thinned her lips. "I'm Detective Parson." She reached over into the box she'd carried in and pulled out a clear plastic bag. "This is motive." She placed the diamond ring in front of Ashley. Parson reached in again for a larger bag. Inside it was Ashley's stainless-steel revolver.

"This is murder," Parson whispered.

Ashley dug her nails into his ribs and he responded by sinking his teeth into her shoulder. He pushed his palm up her back and gripped her ponytail. She felt the tickling strands of her hair lift from her spine and then the taut pull that moved her head back and stretched the skin on her throat. The pain of his bite faded. Ashley loosed her grip on his ribs and locked her fingers behind his neck, pulling her shoulder from his teeth. She held herself, hovering over the floor from the edge of his bed, pushing her hips harder against him. The faint spread of light on the ceiling rolled into darkness as she closed her eyes. His shoulders lifted, and she slipped backward when he relaxed, catching herself at his shoulders. She pulled herself forward and they collapsed against the blankets.

Marshall let out a deep sigh, and his arms swatted against the bed. She rolled to her side, found comfortable support against his bicep and traced a finger over his chest.

"He's being stubborn."

"Be more convincing," Marshall responded, knocking away the dryness of his mouth with his tongue.

"And how am I supposed to do that?"

"I don't know. You're his wife. You should know what makes him squirm."

"Why can't we just tell him?"

"Because then you won't get anything in the divorce."

Ashley walked barefoot onto the tan carpet in the bedroom. Her black leggings hugged around her thighs like a petrified child, the waistband hovering around the bare flesh above her hips. Her stomach was flat, and the peaks of her breasts that were harnessed beneath a red sports bra, pushed ahead of her. The straps clung to her shoulders and hid the bite mark close to her collarbone. Her slender neck curved into a boyish jaw. Her cheeks, scarred with adult acne, flexed as she looked down on Murray. Her husband, wrapped in sleep, packaged in the white down comforter, remained still as she stood at the foot of the mahogany sleigh bed. She'd tied her hair in a ponytail, making her scowl more intense, straining her hairline as she squinted at him. At her side, she tapped the gun in her right hand against the front of her leg.

The gunshot tore Murray from sleep and from beneath the comforter. He toppled from the bed and fell into the narrow space against the wall with the picture frame and his glasses that he cleared from the nightstand during the flailing descent. Murray tapped around the carpet for his glasses, his eyes stinging from the abrupt attempt to focus. Pain grew just above in his forehead and spun—then shredded—through his brain as his eyes took on the light in the room. He caught the earpiece of his glasses when his wedding band struck the plastic and he lifted them to his face between his ring and pinky fingers.

Her silhouette wavered in his vision and he stared at her, waiting for the focus to come in. Every day it got worse, blurred into something submerged. Ashley lowered her gun. Finally, it came, his focus, collecting into form and he saw the details of her posture, the movement of her breathing, the gun in her hand. He looked at the hole in the wall three feet above where he'd been sleeping, then back to Ashley.

"What the hell are you doing?" he asked.

"I want a divorce, Murray." She tossed the gun on the bed where it settled and sunk into the comforter. She folded her arms in front of her.

He took a step forward, out of the narrow space where he stood, scratching his beard. "Aim lower next time," he said as he passed her.

* * *

Murray sat on the floor, leaning against the end of the bed. Ashley had left for her hour-long run. He opened the cardboard box in front of him, something he'd kept in the back corner of the closet. It was only big enough to hold a few of the things from his past, slightly larger than a shoebox. The tape around it had once sealed the care package sent to him when he first went off to college. Murray reached beyond the space where he kept the matching revolver that Ashley had just shot at him, a stupid and awful wedding present from his brother—matching pistols.

Murray continued to look through the box, the coffee mug that read: *We need to talk—God,* that he'd purchased at the Salvation Army for fifty-four cents back when he was a junior in college, after he'd gotten his first apartment and needed things to fill the cabinets and empty corners. That was the year he'd met his wife, Ashley. He dug his fingers through the stack of old letters and envelopes to the bottom of the box and pulled out a Minerva timepiece, the first he'd ever repaired. Murray lifted it to his ear. He looked back up to the hole in the sheetrock. For Murray, timing was everything.

Murray owned a jewelry shop. A tight space in downtown Kennebunkport where most of his business came from tourists during the summer months who bought the clever little artistic jewelry that matched some part of their wardrobe. That morning, Murray hovered over his workbench in the back, the magnifying glass morphing his glasses into fishbowl goggles while he moved the tiny instruments of his profession into place in front of him. He'd been doing this for most of his life, finding the failings in the smallest and most delicate of ornate and elaborate systems. He pulled the case-back off the timepiece and took a moment to look over the still, analogue mechanism.

As Murray removed the small gears and pins, the tiny coil of the mainspring, he thought about the purpose of time, how people wore death on their wrist. The hands moved in a circle, smiling and frowning, chipping away at what was left. Behind the hands, those moving expressions, that's where the true beauty was. Those parts, the mechanism fit and worked together like the syllables of the disease that was killing his brain, him. Murray's eyes strained as he continued, and a headache bore deeper through the center of his head. He finished the repair. The Minerva hummed against his ear, and he saw how he could set the other parts of his life into motion.

Murray stared at the clock above the hutch in his brother's office. The remnants of his headache remained. He heard the faint tick of the clock, but the hands came to him in blurred shadow. Marshall adjusted the placement of the purple gladiola arrangement on the oak hutch.

"It's a lot of money, Murray. I don't know." Marshall turned, sucking at his glaring white veneers.

"Ashley mentioned divorce again."

"And?"

"I'm not doing it. No judge in the state of Maine is going to grant me a divorce without her taking half of everything. Christ, Marshall. You're the lawyer, you know that."

"And what's half of everything, Murray? You're a failing jeweler."

"I'm a horologist."

"You're fucking broke. Your wife wants out."

"If that were the case, she'd file the divorce. She wants money."

"And you don't have any. Cash in on the business, sell the house, get a divorce and start over. I already told you I'd handle the divorce for free."

"Look, I don't need you to handle my divorce. I need you to lend me the thirty-two thousand dollars. If I turn this around, I'll be able to keep the business. Ashley can have the house."

Marshall bit his bottom lip. "And what happens if you don't turn a profit?"

"Then I'll auction the inventory and sign the business over to you."

Marshall finally sat. "You sign the inventory over to me. You can keep the business."

"Deal."

Marshall reached inside his suit coat and pulled out a checkbook. "By the end of the quarter, Murray. I can't do this again."

"I won't need you to. Are you busy this weekend?"

"I'm having dinner tonight at Risottos with a colleague from Boston. I'm considering opening a firm down there."

"Risottos? That's fancy."

"She's a fancy woman."

"Yeah? Attractive?"

"Bombshell. But it's business, not pleasure."

"What time?"

"Eight. Why?"

"I thought you might want to come over Saturday. It's been a while."

"Yeah, well, your place isn't exactly calm these days."

"Tensions run high when your wife is having an affair."

"You don't know that."

"I know more than you think, brother."

Marshall leaned back in the chair then righted himself and stood to readjust the gladiolas. Before he left the room, Murray slipped Marshall's cell phone from the desk and put it in his pocket. He looked back in on his brother who'd already returned to readjusting the position of the gladiolas. Murray looked over at the coat rack, his brother's jacket, and closed the meeting room door. He lifted the jacket from the rack and left.

Outside, Murray looked down the street where it slipped into a barely noticeable descent toward the coast, where the gray clouds miles out to sea were darkening and moving closer. The air was calm, little breeze. The rain was coming. Murray crossed the street and went into the women's clothing store.

Murray slipped through his front door as the rain started, heavy and full in the weight that the darkness of the clouds had promised. Ashley walked briskly into the room before he could wipe away the rain that had fallen on the back of his neck. He shut the door and stood between the brightness the lamps on either side of the door cast through the room.

"Where have you been?"

Murray stared at her. He pushed his hands into the pockets of his brother's jacket. "Looking for reasons to piss you off. I forgot how convenient they are to find."

"Where'd you get that—Is that Marshall's coat? Did you go to see your brother?" Her voice lifted slightly. "Are you going to file the divorce?"

"No. My brother needed something from the shop. I must have grabbed his coat by mistake."

Ashley smiled. "You're so ridiculous. What would he need from that dump?"

"A diamond. He needed it for tonight."

Ashley's smile faded. She raised her eyebrows. "Tonight?"

"Yes. He's meeting some woman from Boston at Risottos around eight thirty. I didn't even know he was dating anyone."

"Interesting."

Murray drew his hand from the jacket pocket. "What the hell?" He looked down at the pair of red lace panties.

Ashley crossed her arms. "What the fuck are those?"

Murray shrugged. "I don't know. They were in the pocket."

Ashley snatched them. She held them in both hands and thumbed over the fabric. She lifted them, put them to her nose and smelled. Murray shook his head slightly.

Her voice came at him lower, almost a growl. "Are these yours?"

"Of course not. Must be one of his many souvenirs."

Ashley squinted. She stared at Murray's chest and it took her a moment to compose herself.

Murray shuffled his hand in the other pocket. "Oh, Christ." He drew his hand out with a small box. He opened it and showed her the diamond. She swallowed, turning her head slightly but keeping her eyes on the size of the stone. "I have to go. I have to get this to him."

Her face was still flushing, and her forearm trembled from the tight grip she kept around the pair of panties. Murray turned and went through the door before she could object.

He stopped and glanced through the window from the side of the road. Ashley was on her phone. Marshall's cell phone vibrated in his pocket. It was Ashley. He hit the button to send the call to voicemail. Ashley threw her phone then picked up the photo frame from the end table and flailed it across the room.

A shadow from the street light loomed over Murray's face from where he sat in the front seat of his car. Water drummed the roof and every few minutes or so, a drop would fall perfectly, hit the edge of the slightly open window and spray a cool mist against his left cheekbone. The side of his beard was moist and the water that collected there had begun to drip from the side of his chin into the gloved hand where he held Ashley's revolver.

Across the street, he stared through the window of the restaurant. He turned his hand to look at the time, check the success of the Minerva. He wondered if Ashley would show, if Marshall had been lying about the bombshell. He wondered if Marshall and Ashley had gotten to the point in their affair that they disregarded public image. Murray had known for a while, since the doctor's visit when he saw her car parked by the wharf and his brother's beside it. Then Marshall stopped coming by the house and Ashley started asking for a divorce. Marshall made his way up the street beneath an umbrella. Murray couldn't see his face, but he could tell it was him by his movement, the way he alternately thrust his shoulders forward while he walked.

Shortly after, Ashley moved slowly up the street. She was drenched, the rain had smeared her hair against her head and shoulders. She still carried the panties in her right hand. The light from the dining room came through the window onto the sidewalk, and Ashley paused there and looked inside. Murray sat up in his seat. When Ashley entered the restaurant, she did it quickly, and almost as quickly as she'd gone in, two of the waiters escorted her out while she screamed behind her into the restaurant and kicked at the air in front of her. One of her shoes, a white flat, flew into the street.

The servers let her go, and Ashley stumbled into the road to grab her shoe. Murray listened to her sob, saw the blurred black streaks of makeup in her face. He'd forgotten what it was like to hurt. Bewildered, much like a few moments before at his curiosity about the details of his wife's affair, Murray wondered why it bothered him to see her so upset, so dehumanized, pathetic. Then he thought about how soon he was going to be able to leave all of that behind.

Ashley put her shoe back on in the middle of the street and walked back toward the restaurant. She lifted the potted plant, an oversized fern, and heaved it through the dining room window. The sound of moving chairs and more shattering glass broke into the night. For a moment, the purr of the rain was gone, but it came back and hushed the noises moving from the restaurant.

Ashley disappeared up the street. Marshall came from the restaurant after that, his white shirt vested with a burgundy wine stain. A blonde followed him and held her hand up to him as he tried to explain. Marshall shoved his hands into his pockets in frustration. The blonde marched away from him and Marshall shambled away down the sidewalk into the breeze that offered a slight chill. Murray tucked the gun into his pocket and followed.

Marshall turned left down a one-way alley, beneath the shelter of a two-foot awning that deflected the rain into the center of the lane. Murray walked quicker, feeling the swiftness of his stride tighten the muscles around his ankles and in the balls of his feet. He felt the blood surging through his arteries. Murray thought about his life up to that point, all the things he'd never done, the rain a cadence to his failures—the business, his marriage, the cancer that was ending his time.

Marshall cursed as he unlocked the door to his office and went inside. He didn't turn to relock it. Murray waited a moment and followed. Inside the first door, Murray pulled the gun from his pocket, tried to decide which hand to use it with. The right? It felt so foreign to him, the cumbersome tool of a labor he'd never known. He put it in his left. Somehow, the awkwardness of his left hand's coordination made it seem a better fit. Marshall's footsteps continued to move down the second-floor hallway to his office. There was the rattle of keys, another door opened, and light nudged toward the top of the stairs. The door closed, and Murray toed his shoes off and made his way up through the darkness.

Detective Parson stood with the back of her hands pressed against her hips. The rubber gloves were a little too large. The fingertips folded against the notepad she held in her right hand. She held her left in a fist around a silver pen.

On the other side of the haughty, cherry desk, the victim, Marshall Jones, lay supine in a leather chair. The back of the chair had fallen against the bookcase behind the desk, and it rested there at an angle, almost teetering. There were bullet holes in the books behind the victim, one in the desk, one in the chair, and one in the victim, just below his left eye. Wild, erratic shooting, Parson noted. She squatted and felt the carpet, the wet spot that had darkened just opposite the victim. The perp must have stood there for a long time.

She stood and reclaimed her previous posture. She walked around the desk, leaned over the victim's right shoulder, moved her face close to the wine-stained shirt and smelled. She paused at the victim's mouth. The lips were open, and she smelled there, too, noticed the burgundy stain in the cracks of his lips. She moved back around, opposite the victim again.

The crew behind her, the other investigators waiting to continue their process, shifted with boredom. She waited a few minutes longer, until muffled sighs joined the impatient shifting. A quick, quiet rumble moved in her stomach and she turned.

The other investigators came into the room. Parson poked around the desk, flipped open the planner and wrote down the name for the eight o'clock meeting time on the previous night.

Parson looked over at one of the other detectives. "Go over to Risottos. See if this is the guy involved in the disturbance they had last night."

She slipped another glove onto her bare hand, stretching her fingers as far as she could into the limp tips of the vinyl and lifted the organizer. She flipped through the pages, every other Thursday marked *A.J.* She pulled a loose piece of paper from the back of the organizer, a receipt from a downtown jeweler for $32,000. She closed the organizer and motioned for an evidence bag. She paused, reached over the desk and rotated the victim's nameplate. She flipped the organizer open again and pulled the receipt.

The next morning, Murray sat at the kitchen table waiting for Ashley. The bulk of the pistol in his waistband ground against his hip bone. She entered the kitchen with heavy footsteps and puffy eyes. The smell of booze trailed behind her. She went to the fridge and pulled out a can of lime-flavored soda. When she cracked the can, Murray glanced at her.

"You hungry?"

She looked at him and took a long gulping drink from the can. "I'm hungover."

"Let me make you some breakfast."

He stood and moved toward her, placing his hand at the small of her waist as he opened the refrigerator door. Ashley frowned as he pulled the carton of eggs from the shelf and looked into her eyes. He bore a cold stare, like he was focused on something emerging from the dark or a distance. She looked away from him.

"I'm going to take a shower," she mumbled and slipped past the hand on her waist.

Murray listened to the sound of the muffled shower in the bathroom. The butter began to sizzle in the pan and he cracked the eggs. While he cooked, he looked through the window above the stove into the backyard. The green foliage and the brown wooden fence melted together in his vision. Murray looked back down to his cooking.

He slid Ashley's eggs onto the plate when the water cut off.

She entered the kitchen a few moments later, and Murray pulled the chair out for her. She looked down at the plate. Murray smelled her shampoo—a deep, velvet smell, dark chocolate. Then, he smelled the liquor. Ashley started her breakfast. Murray broke into a hopeful smile, and he circled the table to sit down.

Ashley swallowed. "It's been a long time since you've made breakfast."

"It's not going to happen again."

"You're a prick."

"I'm dying."

"What are you talking about?"

"I have an inoperable brain tumor. Prognosis was three months."

Ashley lowered her fork. Her mouth parted for a moment, then she leaned back in her chair and stared at him. "Why didn't you say something?"

"I didn't want you to get too excited about the life insurance and stop begging for a divorce."

Ashley scoffed.

"There won't be any life insurance."

"I'm your wife, Murray."

"I'm about to cancel the policy."

"On a Saturday?"

Murray pulled the gun from under his shirt. "I have more surprises for you."

Ashley pushed away from the table. "Murray."

Murray pressed the gun against the top of his ear, heard the Minerva humming. "Watch."

JUST ENOUGH

At some point during the night, I found my way here to Mikey's grave. There was just enough light from the moon to make it on my hands and knees through grass and gravel.

Crawling.

That's really all life is for some of us—moving over one jagged piece of landscape to another from the moment we're born. Even the grass has had to crawl up through the dirt. I haven't been here since Mikey's funeral, when there wasn't any grass. There was just the dirt, looking raw like a new wound just before it begins to bleed. I've propped myself against his headstone to watch another burial.

Someone else I know.

My dress is ruined like the grass beneath me. There's an empty plot right next to this, where I might be buried one day if I should choose to go through that whole ordeal. A funeral, that is. Death isn't an option, only how we die, depending on how lucky we are. Some of us aren't lucky. Some of us try to crawl out of this world by hanging from it.

Like Mikey.

I've been trying to make things right ever since.

Across the cemetery, people are gathered together for Charles' burial, a black mass of swaying and shuddering bodies—bubbling of a tar pit where a body is sinking into the ground. My ruined dress is damp. Wet, actually, because I've been here since I left the bar last night. I only leave the bar when it's dark. When it's safe. The moon drifted across the sky for a while after I first got here, but I fell asleep before it was gone. I woke up to the sunlight seeping over the trees behind me, where it shimmered against the dew on the grass and the headstones and the green tarp they covered Charles' grave dirt with on the other side of the cemetery.

Charles didn't die like Mikey.

Before he was dead, Charles was in a hospital room on the second floor of Sisters of Mercy, and I went by his room with Tina. Tina was my only friend in high school, back when Charles decided that he didn't want any other boys on the cheer squad. Not that it mattered, because boys weren't allowed to use pom-poms on the cheer squad anyway, so I'd lost any desire to join. Tina wore leather jackets and big-heeled boots back then. Nobody ever said it to her face, but *Tina with a wiener* was softly muttered within the walls of the hallway as she passed. Then we became friends, for some reason, and guys like Charles left me alone, except to call me *Tina's Wiener*.

Tina and I stood there, just inside the doorway of Charles' room, while the other next-shift nurses and orderlies were sipping their coffee or sucking down one last cigarette. The sunlight in the room was bright, but not too bright—the way it was before it had a chance to be blinding or hot or anything else that happens to things that start off bright.

Jess came up behind us, the smell of spearmint gum and roasted coffee on her breath. Tina and I met Jess when we first started working at Sisters of Mercy. She saw us out one night, saw me in my silver sequined dress sparkling under a streetlight. A few days later, in the halls of the hospital, she told me she loved it. I'd noticed Jess' clothes. She wore the same pair of jeans to work every day, before she changed into her scrubs, one of three T-shirts and sometimes a tattered gray track hoodie. After our shift, Jess came by my place and I learned that she was a single mother. Her son was very young, and they were on assistance. We spent the afternoon trying on dresses, and despite her attempt to refuse, I made her take a few of those dresses home to keep. Our favorite things have more meaning when we let them go.

In the early morning, there was a musical quality to the noises in the hospital. A sort of melody that built up to sing-song before a chorus came that seemed a little too pretty for the ominous space around it.

When I was younger, I'd heard people in comas referred to as *vegetables*. I never really understood the reference until I saw Charles, plump and motionless at the end of curled tubes that led back to a central cluster. Charles couldn't see himself, but people in comas can sometimes hear what the people around them are saying. I wanted to be clever, have my words slip into Charles' ears the way his did into mine when we were in high school, when Charles didn't think anything was pretty enough for him.

"Radicchio," I said.

"What?" Jess asked. She blinked more rapidly, trying to move into a better state of focus.

"Radicchio. It's a vegetable." I pointed at the mound beneath the sheets in front of us. "Like him."

And then Tina snickered and chuckled.

Jess gave me a confused look. "He doesn't look like radicchio," she said. "More like a butternut squash."

He looked exactly like a butternut squash, but his shape wasn't what I was getting at. "The point is…" I began to say. "Never mind."

"What? He looks like a butternut squash, not radicchio."

"He sure does, Jess. You're exactly right. Thank you for pointing that out."

I had to let it go. She wouldn't understand that I wanted sounds to form shapes in Charles' mind, just like that sensation people feel a half an hour after they hear a comment and suddenly realize it was an inside joke about them. So, I stood there silent until Jess pulled her stare from the corner of the room and left. Tina watched her walk down the hallway.

Tina nudged my shoulder and pointed her chin at Charles. "Rutabaga."

I wondered then, if when they plucked Charles from the vines of his life support, if there would be any glimmer of light, just like that regretful expression people have when they jump from a bridge or a building and the idea seemed better before they realized they couldn't go back. I'd felt like that once, like leaning forward toward the water of a river a hundred feet below a bridge. Mikey had found me. He was the reason that I'd kept hanging on.

Come along, Charles, I thought. Time to die.

I wondered if it would have been better if Charles had fallen instead of dangling in his garage at the end of the steel cable from a come-along that had been draped over a support beam. When people really want to kill themselves, they use more than one method—a gun and a rope, pills and a hose. Charles had high levels of Xanax and Ambien in his system, too, but that didn't stop his wife from coming home early and finding him. She got him here, to the Sisters of Mercy. Sometimes, no amount of planning is enough.

"Turnip," I said, realizing then that he looked a lot more like a soup can under a napkin. And then I thought about how wonderful a bowl of soup would be to ease the nudging hangover from my jaunt at the bar the night before, where I'd decided to go when Tina told me that Charles would be taken off life support the next day.

I'd found tremendous relief in that, that Charles was going to depart this world without ever having the chance to be conscious again, to talk about the things he'd done or the things that had been done to him. And Charles would have talked.

Charles didn't die like Mikey.

Tina and I left the room, stopping by from time to time while we moved through the zoo of heckling patients. When we passed each other in the halls, we'd whisper more vegetable names to each other. We managed to keep ourselves from laughing, but it was a day made almost perfect by our perpetual grins. Some of the patients took notice. Mostly, the ones who were aware that they were dying. And it always took a minute or two for me to realize that I was grinning at a dying person. It made me wonder if they thought I was smiling because *they* were going to die.

I was in Mr. Phelps' room when Charles' family arrived. A small crew of hospital staff led Charles' widow and brother to his room. When Phelps heard their footsteps, he pulled his Johnny up over his genitals. His habit of exposing himself was typically enough of a reason to keep his door closed. When I shut the door, save for a small gap that I could peek through just as Charles' family passed, I realized it might have been more poetic for Charles' family to see Phelps' penis. His useless junk was nothing more than an appendage that made it convenient to piss standing up. Phelps, unfortunately, had lost both of his legs to an infection after his feet had been amputated because of diabetes. I doubt they'd have gotten the connection, Charles' family, that there was one useless dick across the hall from another. One of the nurses slowly closed the door to Charles' room like they were sparing people from having to watch a shitty movie all the way to the credits.

The police had been to the hospital, too, to talk to the doctor. We'd seen plenty of suicide attempts. We knew what looked real and what didn't. People who hang themselves have different bruising patterns on their neck. Vertebrae don't break. There was nothing else in the house that Charles could have used to hang himself. No extension cords, rope or chain. Nothing.

Those details matter.

When Mikey died, the cops had asked the same kinds of questions. He'd left a note, and everyone knew he was gone, but we didn't find his body for a week, even though he'd hanged himself in the woods behind our house. Some people thought he'd just left—packed his things and gone somewhere different. I knew better. The last time I saw Mikey alive, I was working. Charles and two of his friends had cornered Mikey outside of a bar. Mikey wouldn't say anything to the cops.

In some ways, Mikey had it harder than I did, even though I was the one everyone knew was a freak. It's hard enough trying to be the person you are in a world that is always looking for a reason to hate you. Mikey was the smart one. You care a lot less of what people think of you when you're dead.

My father wanted me to work on cars, like him. He wanted me to do other things, too. Things I thought were boy things, like building sheds or splitting firewood or hoisting dead animals toward the rafters in the garage to skin and butcher. I'd protest, grumbling through the process, but I did as I was told. My father knew who I was before I did. He was the first to find me trying on my mother's clothes. It took my mother a little longer to realize, until I was a little too old to be wearing her clothes. She couldn't accept *what* I was. That's what I became to her: a *what* instead of a *who*.

One afternoon, when I was sixteen years old, I met my father in the garage, wearing one of my mother's black cocktail dresses that she couldn't fit into anymore because of how her body had changed after having children. I told him then that I wanted to be a girl and not a boy, that I wanted to do girl things.

He hit me.

He hit me in the back of the head with a limp pair of leather gloves and told me *A girl should know how to work on a car.*

It was my mother who left. The woman who bragged

about all the hard work she'd done for her children, how she managed to keep a home and run her kids around to all their various engagements. She was the loudest woman on the sidelines during youth athletic events. She was proud of her children, me and Mikey. She was one of those people who always wanted to remind people of that—the people at the church and her friends who hadn't or couldn't have children. She was the woman who hung calendars in her home and kept pictures in her office with clever little comments on a mother's love. But she couldn't be a mother to the boy who wanted to wear her clothes. She left with Mikey, who was better at hiding *what* he was. Out of spite, I imagine, she took all of her clothes when she left, even the ones only I could fit into.

The day Charles arrived at Sisters of Mercy, Tina and Jess and I went to the bar and started our night drinking sangria. Sangria reminded me of Mikey. He liked sweet things. We went to the back of the bar at a corner table. Then Tina pulled out a small bottle of whiskey. We passed around the bottle, and while she and Jess winced at the mix of taste between sangria and rye, I just thought about Charles in the hospital bed and whispered *Come along, Charles Dye.*

The irony of his name, the chant that I had remembered from high school, came out as a desperate hope instead of the whispered mutter that I'd repeated during so many hallways wanders back then, when he'd growl *Tina's Wiener* in my ear.

Charles and his friends were drunk one night, and they'd found Mikey at the bar. Mikey felt safe about who he was there. They hadn't been looking for Mikey that night, Charles and his friends, just anyone like him.

But they found *him*. They found *what* they were looking for.

They hated Mikey because he was something that people didn't like—the same people who could forgive a man for backhanding his wife but not a man who didn't want to love a woman. The kinds of people who liked Mikey until they found out why he'd been beaten. They turned their heads. They pointed their hate at how Mikey chose to love.

Mikey should have waited a little longer to go home.

Here at the cemetery, the ceremony for Charles is done. It's time for me to go home, get a hot shower, curl up in my bed now that I know it's all over. There's a pair of jeans and a dry T-shirt in my car that I left in the parking lot behind the bar. It's not too far away. I should get some rest before I go by the hardware store, but I'll never be able to get the sleep I need if I don't go there first.

The brightness inside the store is worse than the searing sun outside. I move through the store with purpose. I don't need any of the men walking quickly toward me to help me find what I'm looking for. At the register, the clerk rests his eyes on my breasts. He looks up, briefly catching my eyes, only to wink.

"This is such a handy thing to have around," he says, lifting up the come-along. Its steel lever and the cable are still shiny, unlike the old one that hanged Charles.

"Oh, for sure," I say.

"I use mine quite a lot during hunting season."

I swipe away a tickle against my shoulder and reply, "My father used his to butcher animals."

"They sure do help to make a hard job a little easier. Does your boyfriend hunt?" He asks me.

"No. I do, though. On occasion."

"A pretty thing like you hunts?" The clerk shakes his head, uninterested in asking me what I hunt or perhaps he doesn't believe me at all. He counts out my change for the come-along and the garden hose.

I've always paid just enough attention to the details to make people believe I'm someone I'm not. I'm not a beautiful woman. And there are some things that I can't hide, but people rarely pay attention to the details. Outside the store, I open my trunk and put my new come-along next to the box of rope and extension cords and chain that I took from Charles' house. I throw the garden hose in on top of that, where there's just enough room for me to close the trunk.

Death is hardly fair, and maybe it wasn't fair to Charles.

But it was just.

Just enough.

DANDELION

The car is parked in the corner of the garage, passenger side tight to the cement wall. Snug. Cozy. Slush and packed snow drop in clumps from the wheel wells. The back windows are tinted so dark, the only way to see through them is to hover at the glass when there's a light on inside the vehicle. The rearview mirror is turned up. The leather seats inside go cold in the sunless corner.

The car's been detailed, but they missed a cigarette lighter. It's white, and it's not yours. Bad luck, you used to say. It probably fell from the pocket of a man with a half-smoked Swisher Sweet behind his ear and his name embroidered on a light blue shirt. Something that ends in a Y, something boyish. Tommy or Johnny or Sammy.

Or perhaps something that begins with a C-L.

Clarence or Cletus or Cleveland.

Names like the men who made you tremble in the flames. The names you can't stop repeating in whispers inside your mind every time you catch your reflection in a pane of glass or in the dark surface of your morning coffee.

The seats are leather because you smoke. But you never

use white lighters. You don't use open flames, only the push-lighter in the car, the only place you'll smoke a cigarette. The leather won't hold the smell, just like parts of your skin can't feel the heat of the sun.

The click of a lighter or the snap of a match makes you shiver, makes your skin burn. Makes you feel like the fire that's still flashing and burning inside you will burst through your skin. The way the flames burst around you inside that barn, where those men left you.

Left us.

But we got away, even though we had to take part of the flame with us, what it left on our skin. The floor of the barn gave out, and we dropped into the pit of water, breathing smoke as we fell, and then the smoke was floating above us, just over the surface of the water. And we wanted to breathe down there, where there was no smoke, inside the water that had wrung out the flames.

You carry that memory like the red-wick ember of a burnt-out candle. You carry it like you held me when the flames erupted around you, where my body fit against yours.

Tight.

The way you tell me to hold my eyes when people see us. When they step back at the sight of our faces, like the flames that touched us will lash out at them from our skin. The way those men jumped away from us after they poured the "holy water" over your head.

They said I'd already been burned, that my nigger skin would just get crispy. Like the fried chicken my daddy liked. And they said you would have crispy skin, too.

But our skin is leather, now. Your skin pale and soft, blending into waxy pink. Mine is still brown, mocha, where your arms had wrapped around me, and where you pressed me against your body.

When you get back to the car, there is snow on your shoulders. It drifts down, floating white and soft until it hits the leather and spreads clear like a teardrop.

You ask me if I'm ready, then help me from the back seat. We walk down the steps of the garage and exit into the night, into an alley deep below the roofs of the buildings that cut slices through the constellations. Near the end of the alley, Jude stands in the light of the doorway. When we get close, he bends down and says, "Good evening, Dandelion."

Jude wears the same clothes he wore last year, his white shirt and black vest. His white gloves are soft and warm. He kisses my cheek and his lips are warm on my soft skin. He kisses my other cheek, and I don't feel his lips, only a tingle in my ear. He holds my hand and I follow him into the building.

We're in the flower shop where you work, and there is a table covered in a white table cloth. There are big shiny metal covers over plates. There are flowers everywhere, surrounding the table, petals soft like parts of my skin. Colors erupting like the flare of the fireworks we watch from a rooftop in the summer.

There is a row of single dandelions growing out of small pots on shelves along the back wall above the table. They are big and yellow like mid-morning suns, but people don't buy them.

Jude helps me into my seat. I swing my feet in the chair while he hands me a big spoon and a big fork, one for each hand. He uncovers the plates after you sit, and there is a piece of red velvet cake with pink frosting.

You watch me while I eat my cake in tiny bites. I want it to last a while, so I can be closer to next year, when we eat cake again. I like the way it feels like a small kiss against my tongue with every bite.

When we're done, Jude takes the plates away. He comes back to the table holding something, covering it with his gloved hand as he approaches. Walking slowly. He sings while he takes small steps, and his voice sounds like an underwater hum.

Happy birthday, you whisper.

Jude puts a tiny yellow pot in front of me and moves his hand from the wish he was protecting for me. The white head of the dandelion is frizzy and soft.

The seedlings tremble against my breath then float up, swirling in the air and floating into your shoulders and around the room.

She had the perfect amount of fear in her eyes. Enough so Ryan knew that she'd do everything he'd told her. They darted beyond him to the pointed corners of the room, where she looked for some consolation for what was happening, what had already happened—some kind gesture or comforting embrace from the truth perching on her shoulders. Each breath Melissa took splintered a sharp ache through her ribs, like fingers had bored their way through the thinner gaps of pain that were already there and squeezed, crushing her into another shape to lift her from the world she knew and shake what life was left in her lungs. Mashed fibers of muscle tingled along either side of her spine.

Ryan noted every miniscule adaptation in her eyes while she thought—a cautious awareness of any movement that came into her vision. He sat motionless, watching her acceptance of where she was, a recycled anticipation of the pain that had already drummed the chorus of a song she was trying to forget.

Beyond her fear, a coiling panic flexed her pupils in the pulsing of the light from the lamp in the corner behind her. The silence in the room began to drone a new noise in her head—blaring static.

Her son squatted between her thighs where she sat on the polyester comforter at the edge of the bed. He'd draped his arms over her knees, the frail seams along the calves of her jeans a convenient cranny for his roving fingers. Sputtering came from his bottom lip, and Ryan looked down at the boy's purple-bruise raccoon mask—the fragments of white tape still on his skin that had bandaged the split in his nose. The woman lifted a shoulder slightly, wincing at the struggle to turn just a few degrees to check the clock again—one minute and forty-six seconds since her last check. Her back was rigid, and the panic in her eyes had drifted, replaced by something else that she didn't have the capacity to acknowledge just yet, but it was him, Ryan sitting across from her on the wooden chair he'd pulled from the desk. She stroked her tongue against the pasty dryness on the back of her teeth.

Ryan reached down to the cuffs of his dark gray suit, perfectly settled on the contour of his body. The fabric was still flat and neat despite the long hours he'd driven, silent, with the boy in the front seat next to him sleeping most of the way. Melissa hadn't slept, hadn't made an attempt to notice the landscape. She just sat in the middle of the back seat watching the road ahead of her. Staring, actually, like she was staring at Ryan's hand. At the edge of his left palm, where his pinky should have been, was a small, mangled bump of flesh. She hadn't noticed until then. He pulled his cuffs down to his wrists, saw her and the child staring at his scar. Ryan stopped his movement and the boy looked up, digging his middle fingers into the holes he'd made in his mother's jeans.

"What happens now?" she asked.

"Now, you live your life." His voice cooed into her soundtrack of static—a raspy, whiskey-scorched voice wallowing in the shadowy room. She focused on his eyes, a placid, motionless depth. Then she looked away, peered at the overlapped edges of beige wallpaper in the corners of the room where they were almost invisible.

"What did you do to your pinky?" the boy asked.

Melissa squeezed her knees together around the child then winced. "Hey, don't be rude."

Ryan clasped his hands together and leaned forward, toward the boy, a flickering patience at the edges of his lips as he grinned. "Gator took it off."

The boy's eyelids retracted, and the cerulean blue of his irises peered up at him. "An alligator?"

"That's right. Chomped it right off while I was walking down the road."

The boy scrunched his face, one eye closing almost entirely, the thin white line of lingering tape bent away from his skin. "In Albuquerque?"

"Yep."

"But there are no alligators in Albuquerque."

"He was my pet alligator."

The boy stopped poking at the seams of his mother's jeans. "Pet alligator?"

"Yeah." Ryan tapped his left leg. "I kept him right here in my pocket."

"Alligators are too big to be in your pocket."

"He was little then, and I carried him around with me everywhere I went."

"Even to the bathroom?"

"Even the bathroom."

The boy turned to look at his mother and whispered, "Can you take an alligator to the bathroom?"

Melissa flinched against the child's movement into the sling around her arm. The finger-length bruises over her neck wimpled when she swallowed. "If it's your pet, you can take it anywhere you want."

The boy snapped his head back toward Ryan. "Where is your alligator now?"

"Well, the alligator got too big to fit in my pocket, so I had to let him go."

"You let him go? Where did you let him go?"

"I let him go in a swamp far, far away from here, where he would have enough space to be with the other alligators like him."

"But why did your alligator bite your finger off?"

Ryan weighed his response against what the boy and his mother had already been through. "Sometimes, the things that we have in our lives hurt us. And maybe they don't mean to, but it's what they do. That's how we know when to let things go."

The child worked his bottom lip back and forth into his mouth, staring at the scar on Ryan's hand.

"Like what my dad did to me and mom?"

"Something like that."

He looked away from the scar to Ryan's face.

"Can I touch it?"

Melissa flexed her legs around the boy's ribs again. "Stop being rude. You don't ask people things like that."

The boy looked down at Ryan's feet. "I'm sorry."

"That's alright." Ryan rubbed his palm over the edge of his scarred hand. At times, human touch felt like the annoyance of flies buzzing around his face. Other times, it made him feel like his skin would peel from his body, tear away like thin fabric and all that would be left would be the tightened flex of muscle covering his bones. Once, he'd let a woman take his hands in a cluttered room when he was drunk on Absinthe in some dank corner of New Orleans. After just a sweep of her thumbs over his knuckles, the woman flung his hands from hers, the hazy clouds in her blind eyes swirling chaotically and she repeated *bokor, bokor, bokor* until he rushed out of there.

He extended his hand to the boy.

The boy looked up at his mother, who gave Ryan an apologetic look, an expression slightly more relieved than the look of worry on her face. She nodded and the boy moved forward to his hands and knees and reached one hand out to touch the scar. The pressure of the boy's tiny fingers squeezed at the gnarled flesh.

"It's cold," the boy said. "Does it still hurt?"

Ryan shook his head. Melissa leaned forward and pressed the forearm of her free arm over her thigh. The boy drew his hand back, a flittering smile on his face. He held his hand up and tucked his smallest digit into his palm. He used his other hand to hold the finger down and observe the four fingers he held out.

"Alright, you," Melissa said. "Time for you to take a bath."

The boy crawled across the dark green carpet on his hands and knees into the bathroom.

"How did you know he liked alligators?"

"I know a lot about you and your son." Ryan pulled a purse and an envelope from the top of the dresser behind him. "Everything you need to know about your new life is in here." He held up the envelope. "Birth certificates, social security cards, résumé—all the things you need to move forward." He handed her the envelope and held out the purse. "In here, your license, checkbook, receipts, a little cash. Day-to-day stuff." He tossed the purse on the bed beside her. "Your back story is written in a narrative so it's easier for you to absorb. You'll want to make that sink into your son's head as much as possible. There are about a dozen pictures for you to keep around. They're photoshopped, obviously, but they coincide with the narrative. It helps with the transition, especially for him. The mind will build false memories. That's all in the envelope."

She flicked the corners of the envelope with her thumb, then placed it on the bed beside the purse, watching her own movement. Her mother had probably found the letter she'd left, which made worry set in about what might happen if someone else found it. "How many times have you done this, *relocation*?"

"Enough to know that everything will be alright as long as you stick to the guidelines I told you about."

"Roy can't find me here?"

Ryan shook his head. "Neither will Victoria."

Melissa rubbed her shoulder. "I never thought I'd live in Oregon."

"The important thing is that you're living."

"What happens tomorrow?"

"Tomorrow you go to your new apartment. A woman named Annabelle will pick you up and help with the rest of your transition. You're safe now."

"Thank you. For all that you've done."

He nodded as he stood to leave the room and looked down on her. "This is where you are, and you can never go home."

* * *

As he left her in the room, he thought about her question. *How many times have you done this?* Never. In seventeen relocations, he'd never betrayed a client, and he wouldn't have, but a week after Victoria Williams' bodyguard Wendell hired him to relocate Roy, they decided to add additional duties to the job. Victoria wanted assurance that Roy would be in the clear for what he'd done. She wanted Melissa and her son relocated, too. The type of relocation that Ryan didn't hire himself out for.

He made his way to the barren interstate that extended east toward the cities he'd already been to, where he'd completed this process before, undoing the ties that cinched the helpless to their mistakes or other terrors they couldn't escape. Despite the hours he'd spent driving Melissa and her son to Oregon from New Mexico, Ryan could still feel the tension in his hands from his meeting with Roy, the smell of the bar where he'd found him—liquor and sweat on Roy's skin, the wisp of chocolate from a protein shake on Roy's last breath.

Ryan had made arrangements through Wendell to pick Roy up at the bar where he worked as a bouncer. He found him outside the door on a chair under the outside light of the bar picking at the thin scabs from the fingernail wounds Melissa had left on his arms when she'd gasped for breath and tried to fight him off. An hour out of town, Roy made the call to his step-mother to let her know that he was safe, that he'd be in touch in a few weeks. When he hung up, Ryan wrapped a thin steel cable around his throat.

Ryan could still taste the dust in the dry air he'd breathed when Roy was beneath him, his knee between Roy's shoulder blades, the cable taut around his hands. He'd wanted Roy to feel how much damage was being done. Steel wire would have cut through, would have made it too quick, and Roy wouldn't have had the chance to tap against Ryan's forearms. As if that was an appropriate call to mercy. Ryan had seen Melissa's back, the eggplant shade of bruising in giant patches the size of continents that Roy's pounding fists left in their voyage. *I guess you can only get it up for your step-mother*, she'd said to Roy before it started. On the ground, Ryan had pulled the life from Roy, let it seep into the air and drift above him, where the vibrant light of the stars shined down on Roy's ending.

If he had done everything he was told, Melissa and her son would be dead, and Roy Williams would be alive, waiting for everything to clear before he could find another woman to damage. If Ryan had done everything he was told, he wouldn't be driving to Dallas to lie to Victoria Williams about what he'd done with her step-son.

In the darkness of the highway, Ryan looked ahead to the sky—the foggy glow of the next city hovering out in the distance. Headlights on the other side of the median crested the hill he was approaching, like glinting eyes rising out of brackish water. He shifted his focus to the white line separating the shoulder lane. The world is nothing more than a swamp full of alligators—motionless predators lurking in murky water that the helpless are trying to wade through.

An excerpt from *Some Awful Cunning*

ACKNOWLEDGMENTS

David, Sarah, Nate, Stephen, Alma, Terry, Anita, Aaron, and Charlie (aka Uncle Squishy). They all know why.

Chelsea, for making my Tuesdays in Ithaca, New York, weird and less sober.

My brother Wesley for the summers, for always helping me get by. My sister Heather for always being the first to offer her generosity. And Matthew, for showing me the challenges and rewards of having a younger brother.

My mother for forgiving the crimes of my youth, the phone calls from jail or the hospital, the tears I caused her in courtrooms, for praying even when she knew it wouldn't do much good, for loving my life despite how reckless I was with it.

Tom Franklin for his patience with my earlier work.

Ace Atkins for my first copy of *The Killer Inside Me*.

Larry Brown and Barry Hannah for their gentle advice.

Christopher Coake for his remarkable efforts to help my transition to Reno as smooth as possible.

Carla Norton for her continual encouragement in my writing.

John Currence for the opportunity to work for him at City Grocery, where I got more of an education than I could have ever received at Ole Miss.

John McManus for his guidance and understanding at Goddard.

My friends from my younger days at Marion Military Institute, especially those who are still in my life, the

Swamp Fox organization there for giving me some direction; my days behind the stick at City Grocery: my regulars, roommates, coworkers and attorneys who did their best to keep me out of jail, or get me out.

Paul Selig and my friends from Goddard who helped me realize who and what I really wanted to be.

For Kamani, even though she can't read this, for nudging me, forcing me to throw the pack on and hit the trail, where nearly half of these stories came to fruition.

JOE RICKER is a former bartender for Southern literary legends Barry Hannah and Larry Brown. He has also worked as a cab driver, innkeeper, acquisitions specialist, professor, and in the Maine timber industry. He currently lives in Reno, Nevada, and spends much of his free time walking uphill.

JoeRicker.com

On the following pages are a few
more great titles from the
Down & Out Books publishing family.

For a complete list of books and to
sign up for our newsletter,
go to DownAndOutBooks.com.

Wear Your Home Like A Scar
Nik Korpon

Down & Out Books
May 2019
978-1-948235-82-2

A clandestine surgeon goes to extreme lengths when she's torn between family loyalties. A con man tries to help his girlfriend escape her pimp, despite what the tarot cards tell her. A drifter hunts down the man who hung her out to dry with a cartel boss. A sicario has a crisis of faith when an old legend stalks him.

From the streets of Baltimore to the comunas of Medellín, the Mexican Sierras to Texas border towns, *Wear Your Home Like a Scar* shows that no matter how deep you cut, you'll never truly leave your home behind.

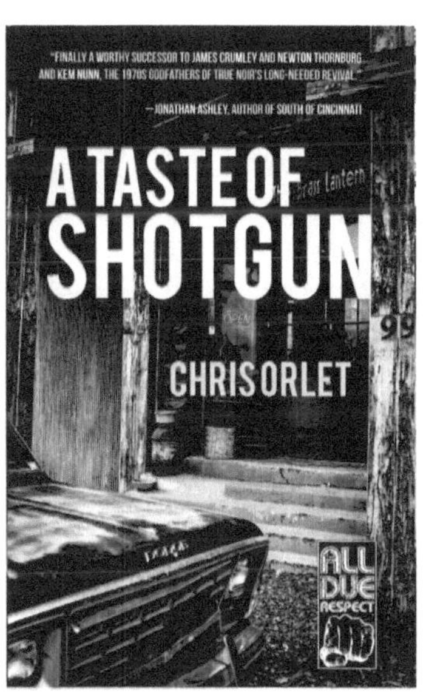

A Taste of Shotgun
Chris Orlet

All Due Respect, an imprint of
Down & Out Books
978-1-946502-92-6

A local drug dealer has the goods on Denis Carroll. That shooting at his tavern five years ago? Turns out the cops got it all wrong. Now, after five years of blackmail, the Carrolls have had enough. When the drug dealer turns up dead, Denis is the prime suspect. As more bodies pile up, they too appear to have Denis' name all over them. Is Denis really a cold-blooded killer or could this be the work of someone with a grudge of her own?

In this darkly humorous small-town noir everyone has something to hide and nothing is at seems.

It's Not My Cult!
A.X. Kalinchuk

Shotgun Honey, an imprint of
Down & Out Books
978-1-948235-71-6

Anthony Dosek, after unwittingly creating a flying saucer cult he would rather forget about, goes to live with his cousin and his wife. Anthony's ruthless second-in-command would rather Anthony not forget his followers, and in trying to create a founder-martyr that will increase cult donations, this wannabe Iago dispatches a cynical former veteran and his naive sidekick to make that martyrdom happen.

In the meantime, to make amends, Anthony tries to reconnect with the mother of his child that he fathered while leading the cult.